With a lazy smile, Seth laid aside the book he held. "What's on your mind?"

"I've learned there's a wounded miner up at Fortymile, and I want to find out if it's Dad. Will you go with me?"

"No, I won't, and I want you to put any thought of going there out of your mind. Fortymile is one hundred seventy miles upriver and certainly no place for a decent woman. It's nothing but a rough mining camp. Dinah, why can't you settle down? You're not a child any longer."

"So you've finally noticed that, have you? Then since I'm not a child, don't treat me as if I am. I thought you were my father's friend."

"I was, and I mourn his disappearance as much as you do, but we have to be practical. You might as well accept the fact that we'll probably never hear from him."

"It will be a long time before I ask you for any help," she said. Tears stung her eyes, but angrily Dinah wiped them away. She slammed the door of his cabin....

BY Irene B. Brand:

GOLDEN PROSPECTS

IRENE B. BRAND

Fleming H. Revell Company
Tarrytown, New York

Scripture quotations in this volume are from the King James Version of the Bible.

Library of Congress Cataloging-in-Publication Data

Brand, Irene B., date
    Golden prospects / Irene B. Brand.
        p.   cm.
    ISBN 0-8007-5406-9
    I. Title.
    PS3552.R2917G65   1991
    813'.54—dc20

Copyright © 1991 by Irene B. Brand
Published by the Fleming H. Revell Company
Tarrytown, New York 10591
Printed in the United States of America

TO the adult choir of Harmony Baptist Church

GOLDEN PROSPECTS

Chapter One

April 1896

"*I*t's now or never," Dinah said.

All winter Dinah Davis had been training her three malamutes as a working team while at the same time conditioning herself to handle the heavy sled. Her skill had to be tested today, before marshy meadows of bluebells, lupine, violets, and mosses replaced the rapidly melting Alaskan snow.

Her dogs, Shadrach, Meshach, and Abednego, jumped and tugged at the rope holding them as Dinah adjusted their harnesses. Smiling at her Athapaskan friend, Jack Crow, who stood beside the hitching post, Dinah stepped lightly on the sled. The malamutes, intelligent eyes shining from masked faces, eagerly watched her movements as she motioned Jack to release the snub rope holding them.

"Mush!" Dinah called.

The initial speed of the three animals rushing along the street took away Dinah's breath. Passing the log school where her father, Nelson Davis, taught, she risked a quick glance and saw him wave to her from the porch.

For five exhilarating miles the dogs sped through the spruce and birch forest, where Dinah often had to duck her head to keep from being knocked off the sled by overhanging branches. The malamutes' black and white coats glistened; their plumed tails waved as their big, well-padded paws churned through the snow.

Leaning expertly to left and right as the sled swayed, she directed the dogs with a few commands: "Gee," "Haw," "Straight ahead." She congratulated herself on the skill of the malamutes and her own successful maneuvering of the sled and dogs.

"I've done it!" Dinah shouted to Jack as the dogs headed for the kennels behind the log house she shared with her father. Once again she'd succeeded at a man's task, proving she could substitute for the boy her father had always wanted. She shouted "Whoa," but at that moment her Persian cat, Bathsheba, skittered around the corner of the cabin, directly across the path of the excited malamutes.

Abednego, the lead dog, who had an ongoing feud with Bathsheba, suddenly changed direction to chase the aggravating feline. The sled tipped sideways and Dinah plunged headlong into a pile of snow. The three malamutes immediately turned on one another, snarling and biting, hopelessly entangling their harnesses.

Without any thought for her own safety, Dinah bounded to her feet and waded into the melee. Jack grabbed a whip and brought it down over the backs of the fighting malamutes just as Dinah felt a rough hand pulling her away from the dogs.

She laughed as she looked up into the face of Seth Morgan, the one man in the village who didn't approve of her tomboyish activities. Gray eyes gleamed as hard as agates from his bronzed, angular face.

"Did you see the smashup?" Dinah asked.

"Yes, I saw it," he said angrily. "Don't you know you might have been hurt badly? When are you going to start acting like a lady?"

Seth aggravated Dinah more quickly than any man she'd

ever known. Her eyes flamed into translucent blue fire as she snapped, "Let's make a bargain: I'll start acting like a lady when you start acting like a preacher."

Seth's face blanched, and he stared at Dinah a full minute before he grabbed her by both shoulders and shook her as if she were a rag doll. Dinah's head rolled back and forth and pain pierced her shoulders from his agonizing grip. At first, his sudden attack stunned her, then she pummeled him with her arms and kicked his shins, first with one foot and then the other. But he towered almost a foot over her, and she couldn't break his grip.

Finally, Seth turned her around, landed a stinging swat on her rear, and released her so suddenly that she fell backward into the snow beside the conquered malamutes. Seth started to turn away, but when he saw that Dinah had fallen, he reached down and lifted her upward. When she staggered, he held her hand, and Dinah put her arms around him to ease her weight on a smarting ankle.

Seth had never touched her before, and while she leaned against his body, drawing on his strength, Dinah experienced a rude awakening. On the day she'd proven she could compete equally in a man's world, she suddenly felt like a woman. Now she knew why Seth Morgan had always annoyed her: She loved this apostate preacher from South Carolina who treated her as if she were a child!

Stung by her sudden knowledge, Dinah pulled away from Seth. "Jack, will you kennel the dogs for me, please?"

As Dinah staggered toward the cabin, Seth caught her arm. "Did you hurt yourself, Dinah?"

Without answering, she shook off his hand and entered the cabin. Knowing she was in love with Seth Morgan brought her no joy. For one thing, Seth, who was twelve years older than her nineteen years, paid little attention to Dinah when he visited her father. Besides, how could she find any solace in loving a man who had turned his back on the God he'd once proclaimed from the pulpit? Love for God was an ever-abiding presence in her life.

For the first time, Dinah was sorry that she'd left Oregon to come north with her father a year ago. If she'd stayed with her grandparents, Maurie and Becky Davis, she wouldn't be experiencing this stabbing pain in her heart. She slumped on a bench beside the table.

" 'Pride goeth before destruction, and an haughty spirit before a fall,' " a woman's voice quoted from the doorway.

"It isn't funny, Susie," Dinah said reproachfully to her next-door neighbor. "I'd had a successful run, and all would have been well if the cat hadn't shown up. That took me by surprise."

Susie closed the door and eased her huge bulk down on the bench beside Dinah. "Let me see that foot. Did you hurt yourself?"

"Sprained my ankle, I think, but not when I fell off the sled. It happened when I kicked Seth. Did you see the way that man grabbed me?"

"Yes. I was looking out the window. What'd you say to make him so mad?"

"I told him I'd act like a lady when he started acting like a preacher."

"Oh, ho! No wonder he shook you. He's touchy about that subject. Remember the old saying, 'Leave well enough alone.' "

Proverbs had tempered Susie's conversation for so many years that Dinah rarely heeded them.

Susie lifted Dinah's ankle and gently massaged it. "No sprain. Looks like it just got an extra jolt when you kicked him." Rising, she continued. "Take off those heavy clothes and stay off your foot. I've got your supper ready. I'll bring it over when your father comes home. He and Waldo should be closing the school soon."

"I don't know why Seth thinks he has the right to order me around. I've a notion to tell Dad how he shook me."

"It won't do any good. You know how even tempered your dad is. He probably thinks you need some chastisement, and he's too soft to administer it himself. Besides, Seth is his good friend."

Dinah had never minded that her one-hundred-pound weight and height of just over five feet made her appear immature. In this female-scarce territory, life was much easier when a woman didn't call attention to her body, especially if it was curvaceous in all the right places. Still, the fact that Seth never seemed to see her as a woman stung.

Dinah consoled herself with the thought that she couldn't have everything. If Seth started noticing she wasn't a girl anymore, so would other men whose attentions wouldn't be welcomed.

Susie, Dinah, and ten other women made up the entire white female population of Circle City, Alaska. The town had been settled only a few years ago, with the discovery of gold on Birch Creek, a stream that ran parallel to the nearby Yukon River. Mistakenly believing the area lay within the Arctic Circle, founder Jack McQuesten had named the village Circle City. The settlement was situated in one of the dreariest sections of the Yukon Valley, overlooking the beginning of the Yukon flats that contained hundreds of swampy islands.

McQuesten owned a two-story trading post at the southern end of town, but for the most part, the town was composed of small moss-chinked cabins that were scattered haphazardly along the banks of the Yukon. Dinah thought it wasn't bad for a frontier town, though, since Circle City boasted a hospital, several stores, a theater, and a lending library. Circle's twenty-eight saloons and eight dance halls presented the debit side. Still, McQuesten touted the village as the largest log town in the world—the "Paris of Alaska."

Although Dinah thought McQuesten's boasts were ridiculous, she liked the village and had enjoyed a carefree year roaming the countryside with her Indian acquaintances and absorbing much of their culture. One of her goals had been to drive a string of malamutes, and she'd just done that successfully.

Before Dinah could leave the main room of the cabin and go to her lean-to bedroom, the door opened cautiously and Nannie Crow, Jack's sister, peered in. Bathsheba bolted in through the open door and eyed Dinah warily as she curled up by the stove.

"I'm mad at you, cat, so you'd better stay out of my way."

Dinah motioned Nannie inside. "Does Jack have the dogs kenneled?"

The lithe Indian girl nodded, her black eyes sparkling. "Also fed them. He say you did good job on sled. Not your fault the cat scared the dogs."

"It's nice of him to say so, but I bet if *he'd* been on the sled, it wouldn't have upended."

Nannie squatted beside the stove. "But Jack has handled dogs since a boy. You've only been trying it a few months."

Nannie and Jack often visited with other native Alaskans living in cabins along the river at the north end of town. It was from this group of Indians that Waldo Knight and Nelson Davis had hoped to entice natives to attend their school, but after a year in Alaska, pupil enrollment remained low.

"Want to work on baskets?"

"Not now, Nannie. Let's wait until tomorrow. I hurt my ankle, and I need to rest."

Favoring Dinah with a slight smile, Nannie nodded. "Don't forget we go to the potlatch and bear dance in a few weeks."

"I'm looking forward to it."

Dinah removed her outer clothing and pulled on a shapeless woolen dress. She peered in a small hand mirror and noted that her curly blond hair tumbled in disorder around her face. The brisk ride through the forest had heightened the color of her normally fair skin. She ran a brush through her hair and returned to the living area of their cabin.

Hoisting her aching ankle to a stool, she thought of home and the many people who'd brought fulfillment to her life. Her mother had died when Dinah was a child, and Nelson Davis hadn't remarried, but her grandmother Becky and neighbor Susie had done a good job of mothering her.

Susie had been a *Hopkins* when she'd come across the plains by wagon train with Dinah's grandmother in 1844, and they'd been friends ever since. Susie had married Stanley Leviatt, one of their wagon-train companions, and after his death, she'd married Waldo Knight, a preacher who'd come to Oregon a few years ago.

Waldo had conceived the idea of starting a missionary school for Indian children in Alaska, and he'd talked Dinah's father into coming with him. Because he'd never felt settled after his wife had died, Nelson Davis eagerly tried a new life. But Dinah could tell he was becoming dissatisfied with the school. Perhaps if Nelson took her away from Alaska, she could forget that encounter with Seth this afternoon.

She hobbled toward the stove and stirred the coals to heat water for tea. Through the window, she saw Seth sliding by on snowshoes, with a heavy pack on his shoulders. He was leaving for his mine on Birch Creek, so she wouldn't have to bother with him for a few weeks. Sighing, she watched his tall, broad body until he moved out of sight behind some buildings.

"Here's your supper," Susie called as she deposited a heavy tray on the table. "I told you to stay off that foot."

Her father entered the room as soon as Susie left, and Dinah limped over to his side. Coming from the cold air into the warm room caused his glasses to steam over, and Nelson groped for the table.

"Let me help you with your coat, Dad," Dinah said as she lifted the heavy mackinaw from his shoulders.

Nelson removed his glasses, and his near-sighted eyes peered at Dinah. "Dogs behave all right today?"

"They did until we got back here and Abednego got wind of Bathsheba."

Without his glasses, Nelson couldn't see more than a few feet, so he didn't notice Dinah's limp. She didn't mention her quarrel with Seth.

Nelson ate in silence, but when he pushed back his plate, he sighed and said, "Only three students in school today. Waldo has decided we made a mistake in coming here."

"But it was his idea," Dinah protested.

"He doesn't deny that, but he expected large groups of Indians to attend our missionary school. He had visions of converting masses of natives. He's discouraged because that didn't happen and wants to close the school."

"He'll probably change his mind again. Susie told me that he wanted to leave almost as soon as we got up here, but he's stayed for over a year."

"Waldo is a restless man. But I guess I am, too, so that's why we get along."

"Does that mean we'll be leaving Alaska soon?" Dinah asked, although the idea brought her no pleasure.

When Nelson didn't reply, Dinah said, "Let me change the bandage on your hand."

She brought warm water and washed off the salve underneath the soiled bandage. Nelson had cut a bad gash in his hand a month ago when he was chopping wood, but the wound had healed nicely. There was only a pink tinge on his skin now, where it had been streaked with infection, but Nelson would always carry the deep scar.

Seth hung his snowshoes on the wall of the cabin that he shared with his three partners in the Birch Creek mine. He unloaded his packs in the empty cabin, opened two tins of tomatoes, and dropped fresh caribou steaks into the frying pan.

His mind was far from this crude cabin in Alaska Territory, however, and as he waited for the food to cook, he wrestled with his problem. Where had that Indian gotten his father's watch? He took the silver watch from his pocket and looked again at the inscription: *Joseph Morgan, April 15, 1863.*

The watch had been a gift from his mother to his father on their wedding day, a week before Joseph had gone north to join Lee's army for the invasion of Pennsylvania. Seth had last seen the watch hanging from a chain across his father's chest, six years ago, just a few months before his father had been killed.

Did this mean that his father's murderer was in Alaska? Could the man he'd hunted for years and despaired of finding be one of his acquaintances? Could he believe the Indian who claimed he'd found the watch in a trash heap near Circle City several months ago? If so, who had thrown the watch away?

Seth mulled over the problem for days without sharing his thoughts with his partners—rough, uncouth men with whom he had little rapport. He couldn't reveal the secrets of his past to them, but he looked forward to his return to Circle City, when he would talk with Nelson Davis about his discovery.

Seth always took at least one meal with the Davises every time he came to Circle City, and Nelson invited him to supper the first evening he returned. Normally this wouldn't have bothered Dinah, but this time she experienced conflicting emotions every time she looked at Seth.

She sat quietly at the table while the men talked, casting oblique glances in Seth's direction, much more aware of his physical characteristics now that she'd analyzed her feelings toward him. Seth didn't have any excess flesh on his six-foot-plus frame. Dark wavy hair crowned a tanned face dominated by deep-set gray eyes. The sweep of his jaw and chin spoke of determination and stubbornness. In the year she'd known him, Dinah had seen him exhibit both traits. Seth intercepted her glance once and flashed a surprised look in her direction. She turned away with a flaming face.

The men lingered over cups of coffee while she washed the dishes. Hanging up the dishcloths behind the stove, she said, "I'm going over to Susie's."

Throwing a parka around her shoulders, she hurried out. When she didn't find Susie at home, Dinah checked the kennels to see if the dogs were comfortable, but the frigid air chilled her body, and she knew she had to quit dallying outside. It might be April, but it was still cold in Alaska.

When she quietly opened the door, she saw that Seth and her father had left the table to sit near the stove, with their backs to her. The popping of the fresh birch log on the fire covered her entry, and with quiet steps, she slipped into her bedroom. She left the door open so the heat from the main cabin could penetrate the cold lean-to. Dinah had every intention of going to sleep, but at Nelson's words, she became alert.

"I've a notion to go prospecting when the weather breaks. With so few children, there isn't any need for two of us at the school. Waldo wants to go back to the States, but I'm not leaving Alaska until I've tried my hand at mining."

"There are lots of creeks that haven't been prospected. It won't hurt to look around."

"That's the way I figure it."

If he goes, I'm going with him, Dinah thought.

Her great-uncle, Matt Miller, had always been looked up to in the family because he'd struck it rich in California. As a child, she'd pretended to be a gold miner, dreaming of all the things she would do if she made a big strike, and the desire to seek gold hadn't diminished as she'd matured.

Once Grandfather Maurie had told her, "Gold mining is

too difficult for a girl. You'd better play at something else, like keeping house, for instance."

With a grimace, she thought of the time she'd gone with her grandparents to visit Matt and Unity Miller in California. That was the first time she'd seen her cousin Vance, who was two years younger than she. He wanted to find gold just as his grandfather Matt had done in 1848, so the two of them started digging in Matt's backyard. They'd dug a sizable ditch before they were discovered, and Dinah still remembered the whipping Maurie had given her.

Lost in daydreams, Dinah didn't realize that Seth and Nelson no longer discussed prospecting until Seth interrupted a period of silence by saying, "Nelson, I have something I want to talk to you about, and I trust you'll respect my confidence."

"What's on your mind?"

"I'll give you some family background and lead up to the problem I have."

Dinah listened with bated breath. Before she'd only been mildly interested in Seth's background, but now she wanted to know every detail of his past. It felt sneaky to be eavesdropping, but didn't she have a perfect right to be in her own bed? She pulled the heavy blankets around her shoulders and settled down to listen.

"I chose a very inopportune time to be born," Seth began. "February fifteenth, eighteen hundred sixty-five, the day after Sherman's Yankees passed through our part of South Carolina and burned our home to the ground. The only buildings left on the whole plantation were slave cabins, and Josh, one of our slaves, and his wife took my mother in and cared for the two of us until my father returned from the war.

"We experienced the same hardships as all other southerners after the conflict ended, but the plight of the black people was even worse than that of the whites. Dad was a preacher, and he did all he could to help the freedmen in our area—an act, I might add, that wasn't appreciated by our neighbors."

"I can imagine. The Ku Klux Klan was pretty active about that time, I hear, trying to take the vote away from the former slaves."

"That's right. Dad preached from the pulpit that the blacks should have equality, which cost him more than one parishioner, but he'd never forgotten what Josh did for my mother and me."

"Took a brave man to do that."

"Yes, and his example encouraged me to be a preacher. He was overjoyed at my decision, of course, and as hard up as we were, he managed to send me to divinity school in Charleston. I was there when he was killed." Seth's voice broke, and several minutes passed before he continued.

"Josh got in trouble with the Klan because he was organizing black voters, and one night when the Klansmen were chasing him, he came to Dad for shelter. When Dad wouldn't turn Josh over to them, they shot Dad and hanged Josh in our yard in front of my mother and little Janice Sue."

Oh, yes, Janice Sue. Dinah tossed her head maliciously. Whenever Seth upbraided Dinah for unbecoming behavior, he always managed to make some comment about how Janice Sue would have acted under similar circumstances. Dinah had grown weary of hearing the name. Noting that Seth had no lengthy praise for his sister this time, Dinah continued listening.

"Even though I had finished divinity school and had been called to pastor a church, I left it all behind to seek revenge."

"As I recall, Klansmen wore masks. How did you know who was responsible for your father's death?"

"For one thing, Josh's son, Sam, watched while his father was hanged, and saw the man's face and heard his name— Leo Cameron, a Klansman from Maryland. Our neighbors, also members of the Klan, were outraged and embarrassed by Father's death, and a few of them told me who'd done the shooting so we wouldn't blame them.

"They said Cameron headed west to the goldfields, so I started out with Sam to find him, determined to make him pay with his life for what he'd done to my father."

"Didn't you find that attitude hard to reconcile with your Christian faith?"

"Any faith I had disappeared when I saw them lower my father's coffin into the grave. Spiritually, I'm as cold as the north wind blowing outside."

"Did you find him?"

"We trailed him to Cripple Creek, arriving there soon after gold was discovered in eighteen ninety-one, but Cameron had already left the camp. I was out of money by then, and I knew Mother and Janice Sue were in need, so I stayed there for several months, prospecting.

"By the time I accumulated enough gold for my family and more to grubstake me, the trail had grown cold, and I gave up. When I heard of this Birch Creek strike, I headed this way. Prospecting had gotten into my blood."

"You haven't been back home?"

"No. I've sent funds to my mother, but I don't want to go back. If I return, I might open old wounds again. And I'd hate to admit that I've failed to find the man I sought."

"Vengeance is a bad road to follow, Seth. Be glad you didn't find the fellow. Two wrongs never make a right."

"If you'd said that a week ago, Nelson, I'd have agreed with you, but something has happened to stir up the whole situation again."

Dinah stifled a sneeze generated by a wave of wood smoke wafting into the room.

"See this?" she heard Seth ask. "My father was robbed as well as murdered, and one of the things they took from his body was this watch. My mother gave it to him on their wedding day, and his name is inscribed on the cover. I found the watch last week."

Dinah sat up, startled. *Was the man Seth sought in Alaska?*

"How'd you find it?" Nelson asked. Dinah wondered why he didn't sound as surprised as she was.

"An Indian had it. He said he found it on the trash heap. I have no reason to disbelieve him, so the man who killed my father is—or has been—in Alaska. All the anger I thought I'd buried has surfaced again. What do you think I should do?"

"Do nothing, man! The way of the transgressor is hard. It's been over five years since your father's death. Even if the man is in Alaska, he's probably changed his name. Forget him. If you start looking for him again, you'll suspect everybody."

"I suspect everyone already. As I walked down the street today, I eyed every person I met, wondering if he could have killed Dad. I feel the need for revenge overpowering me again."

Nelson chuckled. "At the risk of sounding like Susie and her proverbs, I'll remind you of what Solomon said: 'Say not thou, I will recompense evil; but wait on the Lord, and he shall save thee.' "

"The Bible has no power to sway me anymore, Nelson. Thanks for listening, even though you don't agree with me. I'll be treading the vengeance trail again."

After Nelson banked the fire and settled into his bunk, Dinah lay awake, thinking about what Seth had said. How would she feel if someone were responsible for her father's death? Probably the same way Seth did. Could she forgive that person as the Bible commanded? The worst aspect of vengeance was that it often destroyed both parties. If Seth burned with the desire for revenge, no wonder he had no faith.

"God," Dinah prayed, "help my faith in You remain strong. Give Seth the strength to forgive his enemies rather than hate them, and God, what am I going to do about my love for him?"

Chapter Two

May 1896

"No, Dinah." Nelson was adamant in his decision. "You cannot go prospecting with me. I don't want you to speak of it again."

Dinah had nagged her father for days to take her along. Watching as he stored his gear in a heavy backpack, she searched her mind for another argument to sway him. Nelson rarely denied her anything. He'd given in to her pleading and brought her to Alaska; he'd bought her the string of malamutes; he permitted her to run free while he worked at the school.

"I'll miss you, Dad," she said, tears forming in her eyes. "What if something happens to you?"

Looking distressed, Nelson said quickly, as if he were on the verge of relenting. "Now don't start crying. It won't do any good. You can't go. For one thing, you need to help Waldo and Susie."

"With only three students, Waldo can handle the school alone. The Indians will leave for fish camp or their other villages in a few weeks, anyway."

Nelson continued as if she hadn't spoken. "Besides, it's time you start acting grown up. You're nineteen now."

"You sound like Seth Morgan! I'm so tired of hearing about his ladylike sister, Janice Sue, that I could scream. What makes a lady, anyway? And for your information, I'm almost twenty."

"Even more reason for you to settle down."

"How long will you be gone?" Dinah asked as she took a last look at the scar on his hand and covered it with a heavy bandage.

Nelson shook his head. "It could be weeks. I'll not come in until I run out of supplies or make a big strike." Dinah helped him strap the heavy pack over his thin shoulders. Her father had never been physically strong, one of the reasons he turned to schoolteaching rather than a more strenuous profession. But even there, his poor eyesight had been a hindrance.

"Will it be all right if I go to the Indian village with Nannie and Jack for the annual bear dance?"

"I suppose so. Jack seems trustworthy enough. I think he'll take care of you, although Seth doesn't think you should have so much to do with the Indians."

"Seth Morgan's opinion doesn't matter to me. We came up here to teach the Indians, and we can't do that by avoiding them. And I frankly believe the native Alaskans have as much to teach us as we have to share with them."

Nelson appraised his daughter with a look of surprise. "You have a good point there."

"Of course." She waved her arm around the room. "Look at the things Nannie has helped me make. She taught me how to decorate our clothes with beads. I'm learning to make birch-bark baskets now. Jack taught me how to handle the dogs and sled. I've learned so much about the forest, I actually believe I could exist out in the wilds by myself if I had to."

"I hope you won't have to. But to answer your question

about what to do if something happens to me, I've asked Seth to look out for you until I return. So if you run into any problems, talk to him."

Surprised, Dinah said, "Seth? Not Waldo and Susie?"

"Waldo may just pack up and leave on the next boat; Seth isn't going anywhere."

Just what I need—Seth Morgan for my guardian!

Nelson drew Dinah to him and held her close for a moment. "But nothing is going to happen to me. I'll be back in a few weeks. Go with the Indians if you want to. That will keep you from being lonesome. But be careful."

Dinah's tears were genuine now, not a few sniffles to make Nelson change his mind. She would miss her father, for they'd seldom been separated. "*You* be careful. I'll have Susie and Waldo; you won't have anyone. I wish you weren't going alone. And remember, I won't be there to find your glasses, so don't lose them. I wish you hadn't broken your extra pair."

Nelson kissed her on the forehead, picked up his pack, and headed out the door. Rather than mope in the cabin, Dinah ran next door to see Susie. She and Waldo were still at the table, and Dinah plopped into a chair beside them.

"Dad's gone."

Waldo, a man of medium height, whose jet black beard covered most of his face, nodded solemnly. "Yes, he told me he would leave early."

" 'The love of money is the root of all evil,' " Susie said as she placed a hot fried-apple pie in front of Dinah. "I can't believe that Nelson Davis, of all people, would get gold fever."

"I can understand it," Dinah said, "for I've always dreamed of making a gold strike." She shrugged her shoulders. "Anyway, he's gone, and he told me to help you in the school. What is there for me to do?" she asked Waldo.

"Not much. I can handle the teaching, if you'll come by and help with the little ones in case any should wander in.

With these long daylight hours, the children have lost interest in staying inside. I don't know how much longer to keep the school open."

"I'm sorry it hasn't worked out for you, Waldo. You've given it a good try."

Susie's marriage to Waldo had surprised her friends, for Waldo wasn't anything like Susie's first husband, but the marriage had been successful. Waldo couldn't stay in one place long, though, and Dinah wouldn't be at all surprised if the Knights left Alaska before next winter. And if her father hadn't had enough prospecting by then, what would she do?

Wandering outdoors, Dinah found Jack and Nannie, and seemingly most of the population of Circle City, standing, sitting, or lolling on the banks of the Yukon.

"Ice breakup," Jack said.

"Spring is here," Nannie commented with a smile in Dinah's direction.

The Yukon River didn't look any different from the way it had yesterday, but the Indians knew the signs of nature, so she joined them to watch the biggest event of spring. East of the Yukon, snow-covered peaks seemed close by, but to the west and northwest, the mountains loomed many miles away. Circle City sprawled along the Yukon's southern bank for more than a mile, and a dense forest of stunted spruce, tamaracks, and birch trees ringed the town's other borders.

Suddenly, from upstream, a deafening sound reached them, and the frozen Yukon bulged upward as large cracks appeared in its surface. Geysers of milky water spurted skyward from the fissures. Masses of ice, some resembling miniature icebergs, catapulted down the river. Surrounded by muddy water, the ice swayed and heaved from the mighty force of the stream. Several empty boats floundered on the ice floes, and Dinah refused to think what might have happened to any occupants of the boats.

Dinah spent the day watching the spectacle. Since Waldo's

students played with the other Indian children along the bank and watched the ice breakup, Dinah didn't go to the missionary school.

"Go to village soon now," Nannie said. "Are you going?"

"Yes. Will we walk? I need to know what gear to take."

"Go upriver in canoe for many miles, but some walking on portages. We had to wait until the ice went."

Both Nannie and Jack had attended an Episcopal school at Fort Yukon, where they'd learned to speak English. Dinah felt at ease with them, but she had trouble accepting the living conditions and diet of the Indians in general. She intended to take a sleeping bag with her, as well as enough food to last for the week they would be gone.

Dinah hoped that Seth would still be at his mine when they started for the Indian village, but the day before they left, Seth came into Circle City and stopped by the house to see her.

"Heard anything from your dad?" he asked.

"No, and I wish I knew where he was. I'm going to the Indian village tomorrow, and I'll be gone a week."

"You're going by yourself?"

"Why, no," she said innocently, "I'm going with Jack and Nannie."

"That isn't what I meant, and you know it. Sometimes these Indian celebrations become violent, and you might have trouble. As Janice Sue was always taught, 'A lady must always go out in the company of a reliable male escort.'"

Dinah looked at the ceiling, whistling, until he finished his comment about Janice Sue. Sometimes she wondered if he was serious about these stupid comments he made.

"You're talking about South Carolina back in the Dark Ages, not the Territory of Alaska, eighteen ninety-six."

"Rules of good conduct never change."

"Before Dad left he gave his permission for me to attend this potlatch and bear dance, and I'm going."

Staring into the belligerent blue eyes, Seth wondered why he bothered with this rebellious girl, but he did have a duty to his friend Nelson, plus a personal reason for wanting to go to the potlatch. He hoped to see the Indian who'd found his father's watch and question him again.

"Then I'm going along. Nelson told me to look after you."

Dinah's heart beat a little faster, but she controlled her facial features. "I suppose you consider yourself the 'reliable male escort?' "

He grinned at her. "I don't know where you'd find a better one."

Admitting that his presence would make the trip more pleasant, Dinah said sweetly, "Then welcome aboard. I want to learn more about the Athapaskans and their religious beliefs. A little of that won't hurt you, either."

He gave her a sharp, suspicious look but didn't reply.

The birchbark canoe swayed drunkenly under her feet as Dinah settled into the center of the canoe. Seth knelt at the front of the boat, while Jack knelt at the stern. Nannie would ride alone in the smaller canoe carrying their supplies.

The riverbank formed a shallow half-moon with the deepest bend south of town. Sometimes the swampy, level ground around Circle depressed Dinah, who'd grown up with the majestic Cascade Range in full view. Looking eastward to the chain of mountains, Dinah wondered if they'd reach them on this journey.

"Which direction are we going, Jack?"

"South. Yukon flows southeast from here. We travel three days to our summer village."

Nannie had donned her summer costume of moose and caribou skins ornamented with porcupine quills, shells, and beads. Long twists of hair decorated Jack's garments, and with paint he had sketched a black line down his nose, red stripes across the forehead, and red and black marks on his chin. Both Indians had secured their hair with beaded headbands.

As Jack eased away from the bank and into the current, Dinah wished for a moment that she wasn't taking this trip. The swiftness of the water and the swirling eddies testified to the depth of the river. The whitish water marked by glacial silt reminded her of buttermilk. Observing the broad shoulders of Seth made her more confident in the success of this trip, although she admitted that even he wouldn't be of much help if she fell in the Yukon.

The sun was still high when Jack stopped to camp at a secluded area where a small creek emptied into the river. The blackflies attacked them as soon as they stepped ashore, and Nannie hustled to build a smudge fire. Mosquito netting lined the two tents Seth and Jack set up. Without that protection, the pesky insects would rob them of sleep. Dinah was convinced that no other mosquitoes equaled the size of the ones in Alaska.

After their meal, they kept the fire going to discourage the mosquitoes. The setting sun reached the horizon near midnight, illuminating the sky with red hues, and when Jack started a songlike chant, Dinah felt as if the whole universe praised its Maker.

" 'O Lord, how manifold are thy works! in wisdom hast thou made them all: the earth is full of thy riches,' " Dinah quoted one of her favorite psalms aloud.

Sitting beside her, Seth paid no heed to her words, and she remembered that he'd told her father he was spiritually cold. How could he be that way, she wondered, when confronted with the majesty surrounding them tonight?

"Nannie," Dinah said, "tell us something about your people and what they believe about the origin of the universe. The native people of Oregon have some beautiful stories about creation."

Nannie smiled slightly. "Before the coming of the white

man, our people believed that all things had spirits, either on earth or in the hereafter. We believed that animals, fish, and birds took on human form in another life and only appeared as they do in this world to furnish food for man.

"Now our beliefs have been mixed with Christianity, but our shamans still have great power. They can foretell the future, bring about cures. They can also find witches and destroy them and restore lost souls like the *nahani* by praying the demons out of them."

"*Nahani*? What's that?"

"Bad spirits lurking in the forest. They capture the children, bring evil to the people."

"That's what they call anyone who is lost in the forest," Seth commented condescendingly, "so you'd better not get lost."

Dinah gave him a scornful look. "Even if you don't accept their beliefs, can't you at least appreciate the beauty of their culture?"

He shrugged his shoulders and lapsed into silence.

"Are there any *nahani* around now?" Dinah asked, casting an apprehensive glance at the vastness surrounding them.

"One or two, I think," Jack said. "I saw one last winter."

"We have always believed in one supreme being whom we call Lord of the Shining Heavens," Nannie continued, "but Raven is our chief supernatural being, and he played a great part in making the world. He released the daylight, caused the ebb and flow of the tides, provided fresh water to form the lakes and the rivers, and captured fire for man's use."

"Tell of Raven and the flood," Jack said.

"At one time Alaska was completely covered with water. When the flood came, Raven took all the children in his arms and flew toward the heavens. He stayed there until the flood subsided, but when he came to earth, he still couldn't find a place to land. He called upon his friend Frog for help. Frog rose to the surface of the water and let Raven light on his back, and thus the children were saved."

"Is Frog supposed to represent Noah and his ark, mentioned in the Bible?" Dinah wondered aloud.

"I do not know," Nannie said. "I didn't hear of Noah until I went to school at Fort Yukon."

"How could these natives have learned stories that are similar to our Bible, Seth?"

Seth shrugged his shoulders again, seemingly reluctant to discuss spiritual subjects.

"I believe God revealed His truth to them, and they've woven the revelation into these symbolic tales to explain what they couldn't understand," Dinah said.

"Believe what you want to."

The next morning when they started, Dinah said, "Let me paddle today, Jack. I want to learn how it's done."

He nodded. It seemed strange to Dinah that Jack had never questioned whether she could accomplish whatever she set out to do.

"I paddle, too," he said. "You sit in front. I paddle from stern. Seth must sit in the middle."

Jack handed Dinah a shorter paddle than the one he held. "You'll find it more comfortable to sit, I think." Yesterday, Dinah had noticed that Jack frequently changed positions from sitting to kneeling. "Hold the paddle like this, one hand near the top and the other hand near the blade. Keep your hands as far apart as the width of your shoulders. Draw paddle through the water by pulling back with the lower arm and pushing forward with the other."

Feeling bewildered, Dinah said, "Maybe I'd better not try it."

"Nannie can do it; so can you, but not for long. You'll get tired. Try awhile and then rest."

When they reached the river current, the canoe lurched and spun around in circles. Dinah looked fearfully over her shoulder at Jack, and he encouraged, "Watch this." After a few more tries, Dinah fell into the rhythm that Jack set, and the canoe shot forward.

Seth's face had clouded when he was relegated to the role of passenger while Dinah helped propel the canoe upstream, and he hadn't said a word since. But Dinah was too concerned with paddling the canoe to worry about him. She soon learned the strokes necessary to move the craft, but in a short time her arm felt as if every muscle were being pulled loose. Sensing Seth's disapproval, she gritted her teeth and kept going.

After about an hour, Jack pulled over to the bank. "Enough now. You can paddle again this afternoon."

Her second try was easier, but when they stopped for the night, Dinah's arms ached so much that she couldn't sleep. Perhaps sensing that Dinah didn't want Seth to know she suffered, Nannie took no notice until they sought their tent. Then, quietly, the Indian girl massaged Dinah's aching muscles and rubbed them with some foul-smelling ointment.

"You're a good friend, Nannie," Dinah whispered.

Although she still had some aches, Dinah insisted on paddling again the next day. Before they settled in the canoe, Jack eyed Seth. "Want to try?" he asked, holding up the paddle.

Seth hesitated for a moment. "No, thank you. One amateur canoeist is enough."

"In other words, Seth Morgan, you're afraid you can't handle the boat as well as I can."

"It wouldn't take much skill to do that," he retorted.

By late afternoon, Jack turned into a small creek emptying into the Yukon. "Good idea for you to practice paddling in the small stream. Much easier to learn here than in the Yukon. You did good, though."

"Thanks, Jack," Dinah said, favoring Seth with a pert look.

As they rowed easily along the placid creek, Dinah encouraged Jack to talk about the village they would visit. Jack and Nannie belonged to the Han group of the Athapaskans, numbering a few hundred Indians scattered throughout eastern Alaska and the Yukon Territory.

They reached their destination along the bank of the small creek in a few hours. Jack explained that the portable dome-shaped moose-skin tents had been constructed out of curved poles. At their winter village, the structures, about fourteen feet in diameter and eight feet high, were heavily insulated with evergreen boughs. Heavy snows also kept heat inside the dwellings. Although these tents were portable, at their summer fish camp and for the fall hunts, the Han used smaller tents.

Nannie invited Dinah to share the home of her parents, but Dinah had no wish to sleep in one of the crowded dwellings. Near the creek bank, she erected the small tent they'd used on the trip upriver, and Dinah hurried inside to escape the mosquitoes. Seeing that Seth occupied the other tent not far from hers gave Dinah a feeling of security, although she wouldn't have admitted it to him.

Not wanting to miss any of the festivities, Dinah rubbed an oil Nannie had supplied on her face and hands and ventured toward the village.

"Wait up," Seth called. "What's going on tonight?"

"They have a bear dance, Nannie says, before the potlatch. I think the celebration lasts for several days."

"Not many, I hope. I can't stay here a great while."

"The dance combines religious and practical motives. This is supposed to be the same kind of dance the bears perform when they come out of hibernation. If the natives can gain the bears' friendship by having this dance in their honor, when it's necessary for the Indians to hunt them, the spirits of the bears have been conciliated."

The Indians crowded in trees and on high benches above a large circle bordered with brush, the women on one side of the circle, with the men facing them. Jack motioned to Seth and Dinah when they reached the clearing and helped them climb to a high perch.

"We've got a bird's-eye view from here. Hope we don't fall off," Dinah said.

A warrior wearing an eagle mask gave a dance of greeting. He accompanied his steps with the beating of two globular rattles held in each hand and the beating of a large, flat, double-headed drum hung from four stakes. The dancer moved from a deep crouch into a slide step, circling to the left. As the tempo of the song changed, the dancer lifted his arms, bent at the elbows and held shoulder high to represent the wings of the eagle. He jumped into the air, both his feet struck the ground together, and he shifted his weight from one foot to the other. After going through this routine several times, he reverted to a crouch, then ran from the circle.

"Not bad!" Seth said. "This may be a better experience than I thought."

"It's not difficult to tell this is the bear dance," Dinah commented when the drumbeats increased in volume and several men covered with bearskins entered the circle. They growled, dug into the ground with their bare hands, and paced around the circle, jumping at the onlookers. One bear ran out of the circle but soon returned holding a dead rabbit in his paw. The other bears advanced on him, trying to take the rabbit, and when one succeeded, he skinned the rabbit and ate some of the raw flesh.

Dinah's stomach crawled, and she gasped. Seth reached for her hand and held it tightly.

When the bears left the area, the women marched across the open space and chose dancing partners. With arms locked, the women waited while the men clasped hands and faced their partners. The movement of the dance consisted of two long steps ahead and three short ones back, alternating on each foot. The performance involved a series of advances and retreats on the part of the two lines.

"Pretty simple, isn't it, when compared to the waltz and square dancing?"

Dinah agreed. "But I can still appreciate the beauty of their movements, for the steps harmonize with their culture. You'll have to admit that waltzing would seem out of place here."

Seth laughed. "Guess you're right."

Dinah sighed inwardly. Seth could be the best companion most of the time, especially when he wasn't trying to reform her.

"I'm glad you came along, Seth," she admitted. "I'd have felt lonely with only the Indians."

He squeezed her hand.

The dancing continued all the next day until sunset, when a feast was served.

"The big giveaway takes place tomorrow, and then we can leave for Circle," Dinah told Seth as they sampled the strange-tasting food.

"I understand that chiefs plan these potlatches a year or so in advance."

"Nannie says it takes a long time to prepare enough food and provide items to give away. The person who hosts the potlatch is usually destitute when the day ends."

"He'll get it back next year when some rival chief tries to outdo the first chief's generosity."

Pointing to the stack of blankets, baskets, and bags full of many useful items beside the chief's dwelling, Dinah said, "This bounty will be difficult to match."

Not wanting to miss any of the distribution of goods, Dinah and Seth were on hand early the next morning. The chief stood beside the pile of gifts with a shield-shaped copper piece around his neck and a holstered pistol at his waist. As they walked close to the chief, Seth stopped suddenly and grabbed Dinah by the arm.

"What's wrong?" she said.

He dragged her across the circle, away from the Indians. "I've got to think a little. That Indian is wearing my father's pistol." Briefly, he repeated much of what he'd recently shared with her father.

"That pistol and the watch were the two items taken from my father's body. Whoever killed him has to be here in Alaska. Just when I thought I could settle down and forget my sorrow, these two things crop up."

"You'd better forget the idea of revenge. You know that Indian didn't kill your father."

"No, but he might lead me to the one who did." When Jack approached them, Seth said, "Will you ask the chief where he got the pistol he's wearing, and if he'll sell it to me?"

Jack nodded, and they followed him into the dancing circle. After hearing Jack's question, the chief launched into an outpouring of words in his native tongue.

"Priest man had the gun, and he can't sell because he's giving away all of his possessions. Gun must go," Jack reported.

"If I give him my rifle in exchange, wouldn't that be as good? I know he doesn't have bullets for the pistol, but he could use the rifle."

When Jack relayed the message to the Indian, he muttered something, and Dinah thought he must be relenting. "See gun," the Indian said, and Seth hurried toward his tent. While he was gone, Dinah looked closely at the gun, and she could see why Seth had recognized it. The old-style pistol had an eagle carved in the wooden handle, as well as the initials *AMM*.

Seth demonstrated the rifle to the Indian and handed him a bag of shells. Reluctantly, it seemed to Dinah, he gave Seth the pistol. Once the pistol was in his hands, Seth headed for his tent, and Dinah followed him.

"The initials are my grandfather's, Ambrose Manford Morgan. He carried this gun through the War of 1812 and gave it to my father when he entered the Confederate army. I'm glad to have it back in the family."

"How do you think it happens to be here in Alaska?"

"All I could get out of the Indian was 'priest man had,' and that could mean anything."

"There's a priest in Circle City by the name of Father Judge. Maybe the Indians stole it from him."

"I know, and he comes to these villages, but I hardly think he would have a gun. I'm friendly with Father Judge, and I'll question him. It's a mystery, but I intend to unravel it someway. I can't go on carrying this burden forever."

Chapter Three

Summer 1896

*D*inah eagerly opened the door of their cabin, looking for signs that her father had returned while she was at the Indian village. Bathsheba purred a welcome, and Dinah stopped to rub the feline's arching back, but disappointment surfaced when she realized the room was just as she'd left it.

"Maybe Susie or Waldo will have heard from him," she muttered, but she checked herself from going next door to their cabin. They'd be asleep at this hour.

Flinging her packs on the kitchen floor, she went to the kennels to check the dogs. Curled into round balls, they were sleeping, so she returned to the cabin. She settled into bed, but not to sleep. Their experiences at the Indian camp rolled through her head. She and Seth had been more companionable than ever before, and at times, she had considered telling him of her love. The fact that they'd shared in the discovery of his father's gun had forged a bond between them.

But his thirst for revenge had also caused restraint. How could a man who'd studied for the ministry forget all the biblical admonitions about loving your enemies and forgiving them? Dinah had tried to reason with Seth about his attitude, but when she saw it angered him, she said nothing more. The week they'd shared had been so wonderful that she didn't want to spoil their last days by quarreling. She could pray, though, that he would see the futility of searching for his father's assassin. As long as he didn't know about her prayers, he couldn't argue with her about them.

Worry about her father and Seth's problem discouraged sleep. She had hoped that Nelson would have returned by now and given up his gold seeking, so they could. . . . *Could do what?* What if Nelson decided that he'd had enough of Alaska and returned to Oregon? Could she leave Seth now?

Dinah hurried out of bed when Susie entered the cabin early the next morning.

Susie had the fire lighted by the time Dinah dressed.

"Morning, Dinah," she said. "What kind of time did you have?"

"Interesting, but their customs seem strange. I even learned to paddle a canoe. Jack and Nannie are good teachers. Have you heard from Dad?"

Setting a plate of biscuits and a slab of caribou meat in front of Dinah, Susie said, "Never face a problem on an empty stomach. Eat your breakfast, and we'll talk later."

Dinah cast a speculative glance in Susie's direction, but she ate the food with relish, for her provisions at the Indian village hadn't lasted as long as she had anticipated. When she pushed her plate aside and poured another cup of coffee, she turned to Susie. "I'm finished."

"I didn't want to give you bad news on an empty stomach."

"Bad news about Dad!"

"Looks like it might be. A couple of hunters came upon his camp in the hills. They spent one night with him, but when they circled back two days later, he was gone. His camp stuff was still there, and they settled down for the night, but

Nelson didn't come in. They hunted again that day, came back in the evening—still no Nelson."

"Maybe he set up temporary quarters in another place."

"That could be, so I don't think there's any big reason for alarm, but you had to know. The two men came on into Circle thinking he might be here."

"I wish I'd made him take me along. I know I could have, if I'd insisted." She knew why she hadn't. Seth wouldn't consider it refined for a woman to live in a prospector's camp, and she desired his good opinion more than she once had. She had to stop being so foolish; she couldn't let Seth's values dominate her life.

"Don't worry about it, Dinah. I imagine he'll show up in a few days. 'No news is good news.' "

But a month went by without news of Nelson Davis. Dinah tried to take an interest in basket weaving. She exercised her dogs daily to increase her skill in handling them. Nights were the worst. She couldn't sleep, wondering what had happened to her father.

She pestered Seth until he finally went to the campsite and brought in Nelson's gear. He'd gone without telling her, angering Dinah because he hadn't taken her along.

With a brief "thanks" in his direction, Dinah ignored Seth while she opened the pack and looked slowly at Nelson's equipment. Very little of his food had been eaten.

"I threw away the bacon and butter. They were rancid."

"Seth!" Dinah cried as she lifted Nelson's glasses from the heap.

Seth's eyes were compassionate, and he put his arms around her. "I know, Dinah. I considered not letting you see them."

"But he can't see a foot in front of his face without these glasses. No wonder he hasn't come to camp. He can't find his way."

"Yes, but why would he go away without them? He couldn't see then, either."

"He's always left his glasses lying around, and I'd have to find them for him. Seth, go with me into the hills. He may be wandering around lost." She clutched his arm. "Please, Seth."

He dropped his arms and moved away from her. "Dinah, there's no use. I've spent two days looking for him. He is not near that camp, and I have to go back to the mine."

Determined not to give up, Dinah enlisted help from Nannie and Jack, and for weeks the three of them patrolled every stream in the vicinity of Circle City and Birch Creek. By the first of August, she had to accept the truth: Nelson Davis had disappeared without any sign.

Dinah dragged wearily into the Knights' cabin to report her failure. Susie drew Dinah into her arms and said, "Dinah, I hate to tell you this now, but we're planning to leave Alaska before the freeze-up and go back to Oregon. I think you should go with us."

"Oh, no! I can't leave until I know what happened to Dad. Please don't go yet!"

"Waldo has pestered me to leave since the Indian children went to fish camp, but I've been holding him off. He can't see any reason why you can't go along, but then he hasn't known you as long as I have. It's best to 'let sleeping dogs lie,' he thinks."

"Susie, I'm not leaving Alaska until I hear from my father. I couldn't face my grandmother if I deserted him."

With a grimace, Susie said, "That's bothering me, too. How do you think I can face Becky if I leave you up here by yourself?"

"I'll send her and Grandpa a letter and tell them I refused to come and not to blame you."

"Dinah, I'm being pulled two ways. Waldo is awfully anxious all of a sudden to leave the territory, but I also want to know what happened to Nelson. I'll hold him off until the middle of September, but we can't wait any longer than that, or winter will catch us."

The next morning, Dinah heard a slight tap on the door, and Jack stood on the threshold. "News came in from Fortymile about a wounded man found by riverside. Could be your father?"

"Maybe it could, Jack," Dinah said, new hope surging into her heart. "Thank you. Seth is in town now. I'll see if he'll go with me to check it out."

Dinah pushed the pan of beans to the back of the stove and hurried to the small cabin Seth occupied when he was in Circle City.

"Come in," he called when she knocked on the door.

One wall of the cabin was lined with shelves containing several volumes of books. Seth probably had more books than the lending library in Circle. Caribou and moose antlers decorated the other walls. Colorful blankets lay across the chairs and on his cot. Birchbark baskets held his possessions. The cabin was as neat as her own. *What a talent this man is wasting in this wilderness!* she thought. Seth had a brilliant mind that shouldn't be sacrificed to digging a shovelful of gold out of the earth. But he hadn't asked for her advice and wouldn't have taken any she proffered.

With a lazy smile, Seth laid aside the book he held. "What's on your mind?"

"I've learned there's a wounded miner up at Fortymile, and I want to find out if it's Dad. Will you go with me?"

"No, I won't, and I want you to put any thought of going there out of your mind. Fortymile is one hundred and seventy miles upriver, and certainly no place for a decent woman. It's nothing but a rough mining camp. Dinah, why can't you settle down? You're not a child any longer."

"So you've finally noticed that, have you? Then since I'm

not a child, don't treat me as if I were. I thought you were my father's friend."

"I am, and I mourn his disappearance as much as you do, but we have to be practical. You might as well accept the fact that we'll probably never hear from him."

"It will be a long time before I ask you for any help," she said. Tears stung her eyes, but she angrily wiped them away. She slammed the door of Seth's cabin, stomped to the southern end of town, and found Nannie and Jack in the Indian village.

"Seth has refused to go with me to Fortymile. If I try to leave now, he'll enlist the help of Waldo and Susie to keep me here, and I'll be outnumbered. Keep watch, and as soon as he goes back to the mine, if you'll go with me, we'll travel to Fortymile by ourselves."

Seth stayed in Circle for two more days while Dinah fidgeted in her cabin, but early on the third morning, Nannie tapped at her door.

"He's gone. We can go right away."

Leaving a note on the table for Susie, Dinah shouldered her packs and followed Nannie down to the Yukon's bank, where Jack waited in his large canoe. Nannie and Jack took the paddles at first, but Dinah did her share, and they endured ten days of hard travel before they beached their canoe in front of a hodgepodge town of log buildings strewn carelessly along the mud bank where the Fortymile River emptied into the Yukon. Stumps, piles of discarded pay dirt, tin cans, and wood shavings scattered on the surrounding marshland combined to make the town one of the ugliest places Dinah had ever seen.

With Jack at her heels, Dinah walked briskly through the town, avoiding the eyes of the curious miners lounging in front of numerous saloons and dance halls. Riveting her attention on the British flag in the distance, she finally came to a medium-sized cabin on the outskirts of town. The sign,

NORTH WEST MOUNTED POLICE, indicated she'd arrived at the place she wanted.

Jack settled down on the steps, and Dinah went inside. The young Mountie behind the desk rose with a delighted smile.

"Corporal Timothy McCormick at your service, ma'am. What can I do for you?"

Dinah felt her throat constrict, and she feared she might give way to tears. The past few days had taxed her strength, but her tension eased at the sight of his friendly blue eyes and the pleasant face crowned with wavy blond hair.

He scurried around the desk and offered her a chair that she took gratefully.

"I'm Dinah Davis, and I live at Circle City. My father disappeared about three months ago, and we've had no word from him. I heard there was an unidentified wounded man here, and I want to know if it's my dad."

Sympathy softened the Mountie's eyes, and he said, "I'm sorry to inform you, Miss Davis, that the man died this morning. He hasn't been buried yet, and you can see him, but I'm afraid it will be bad news for you either way. Come with me. His body is in a building out back."

McCormick took Dinah's arm and led her toward a small cabin with bars over the windows behind the main headquarters. She hesitated on the threshold. Why couldn't Seth have come with her so she wouldn't have had to endure this experience alone? Why did she persist in loving such an inconsiderate man?

Perhaps sensing her trauma, McCormick said, "If you'll give me a description of your father, I might be able to tell if this is the right man. Did he have any distinguishing marks?"

"My father is tall and thin. His hair is mostly gray. He has a recent scar on his right hand."

"This man wears a beard, and I don't consider him tall. His hair is brown. So it probably isn't your father, but I expect you'll be more content if you see for yourself."

Dinah clutched Timothy's arm as he led her toward the cot. She closed her eyes when he reached for the blanket that covered the body. In a way she hoped the man was her father; at least she'd know what had happened to him. She finally opened her eyes and stared at the emaciated body on the cot. This man with such distorted features wasn't Nelson Davis. Her gaze traveled the length of his body and rested on his right hand. No scar! She released her breath in a long sigh.

When Timothy led her back into the sunlight, Dinah said, "In a way I'm relieved, of course, but I'm still left with the mystery of what happened to my father."

"Miss Davis, surely you didn't come here alone?"

"No, Jack and Nannie Crow, Han natives, came with me. They're my good friends."

"Will you be our guest while you're here? We have an empty cabin belonging to a Mountie who returned to Ottawa. You're welcome to stay there."

"Thank you. I'll accept your hospitality. We had a strenuous voyage upriver from Circle, and I do want to rest a few days before we return."

"In the meantime, I'll make inquiries about your father."

Dinah felt much more relaxed when she walked back toward the river, with Timothy's tall form beside her and Jack following them. When they arrived at the canoe, Timothy shouldered her pack.

"Will it be all right for Nannie to stay in the cabin with me?"

"That's up to you, Miss," Timothy said, but his tone wasn't hospitable.

"No, I'll stay here at the canoe with Jack. Not safe for us to leave the canoe unattended."

"Check with me every day, will you? I'll want to return to Circle soon."

*   *   *

Thankful that she'd had the foresight to bring along one good dress, Dinah bathed in the warm water provided by an Indian servant. The blue garment set off the gold of her hair, and her blue eyes gleamed from skin that had darkened during the Alaskan summer. *Grandma Becky wouldn't recognize me now*, Dinah thought. Although she'd never have Becky's beauty that her grandfather boasted about, she thought she looked good enough as she left the cabin and went toward the main office where she was to dine with the Mounties.

Three men leaped to their feet as she entered the room, and Timothy made the introductions. The thickset graying man was Charles Constantine, the officer in charge of the detachment. Bill Ogilvie, not in uniform, was introduced as a government surveyor. During their meal, Dinah learned that the Mounties at Fortymile numbered twenty, but that many of the officers were presently on patrol duty in the area.

Dinah enjoyed the food served on real china with silver utensils, and she also appreciated the admiration of the three Canadians. The men at Circle City had grown so used to her mannish activities that they hardly gave her a glance, but these men, apparently starved for female companionship, hung on her every word.

While they lingered over cups of tea, a knock sounded on the door, and a bearded man entered at Constantine's invitation.

"Mr. Ogilvie, wonder if it'd be too much to ask you to come to McPhee's Saloon? George Carmack's down there. Claims he's made a strike on Rabbit Creek. We ain't sure his stuff is genuine."

"Carmack? Isn't he that squaw man who lives with the Tagish tribe?" Constantine asked, disapproval in his tone.

"Yeah. He's got two of the Injuns with him now. They was in on the strike. They've staked claims on the creek, registered them at Fort Cudahy, and have come to pass the news. But even if the dust is good pay dirt, we ain't sure he didn't find the gold in one of the creeks around here."

Ogilvie stood up. "I'll take a look. Want to come along?" he said to Constantine and Timothy.

"If Miss Davis will excuse us for a few minutes, perhaps we'd better," Timothy said, and with an apologetic glance at Dinah, he continued, "These miners get excited when they hear about a strike."

"Of course. Go right along," Dinah said, her heart pounding with strange excitement. She waited for a few minutes after the men left the cabin, then grabbed a blanket that she draped over her head and shoulders before slipping out the door. She'd noticed McPhee's Saloon earlier when they'd walked along the street, and she thought she could find it.

No one noticed when Dinah slipped inside the crowded saloon, because all eyes focused on a white man and two Indians talking with Ogilvie at the bar.

The white man with the heavy jowls, sleepy eyes, and plump features, whom Dinah took for Carmack, held aloft a tobacco can. "Yes, sir, I found a big claim," he said. "A few of us were hunting up the Klondike, and we saw some color in Rabbit Creek. We dug around for a few minutes and came up with a lot of gold. I staked two claims as my right of discovery, and Skookum Jim and Tagish Charley took out single claims."

A handsome giant of a man, Skookum Jim had an eagle nose and fiery black eyes that appraised Carmack. His companion, Tagish Charley, wasn't so handsome, but he was lean and lithe as a panther.

Skookum Jim looked at Carmack with scornful eyes and said, "I made discovery. Carmack was asleep under a tree when I scooped up the first pan of gravel. But white man wouldn't let Indian claim discovery."

"What about it, Ogilvie? Is it a new claim?" the man behind the bar said.

Ogilvie peered intently at the nuggets in his hand. "I'd say so, men. I've never seen nuggets like this before. They've come from a new location."

Pandemonium erupted in the room. Men shouted, threw their hats in the air, and pounded the backs of Carmack and the two Indians.

"The drinks are on me, boys," Carmack shouted, dumping the contents of the can on the bar. "There's plenty more where this came from."

When the miners surged toward the bar, Dinah slipped quickly from the saloon. At the river, she found Jack and Nannie huddled around a fire to ward off the mosquitoes.

"What's all the excitement?" Nannie asked.

"Did you ever hear of George Carmack?"

Jack nodded. "Squaw man. Lives with Tagish tribe."

"He's apparently made a gold strike on Rabbit Creek. You know where that is?"

"About thirty miles upstream."

"I want to go," Dinah cried excitedly. "This may be the only opportunity I'll ever have to prospect for gold. Will you go with me?"

"Don't care about gold," Jack muttered. "Bad for people. But I'll take you."

Excited men poured in droves from the saloon. "We'll have to hurry. I'll bring my pack from the Mounties' barracks. As light as it is, we can make many miles before morning."

Everyone else seemed to have the same idea, for several loaded boats were already moving upstream.

Seeing Timothy McCormick on the steps of his cabin, Dinah rushed over to tell him good-bye.

"Thanks so much for your hospitality, sir, but I'm heading up the Yukon with the others. I've always dreamed of finding gold."

Dinah stifled a laugh at his bewildered expression. "But, Miss Davis, you're lady!"

"I'll remain a lady, but hopefully a rich one."

She ran down the street before he could stop her. Seeing Bill Ogilvie on the steps of McPhee's Saloon, she paused. "How do you go about staking a claim, Mr. Ogilvie?"

He gaped at her for a few moments. "Claims range from rim rock on one side of a creek to rim rock on the opposite side. Each claim can be two-hundred-fifty feet wide. Step it off correctly, drive in wooden stakes, and write your name on them. It's my job to record and inspect all the claims to be sure the boundaries are right. If you stake a claim, come back here to record it." Taking in at a glance the teeming humanity around them, he cautioned, "But, Miss Davis, I don't think you should go."

"There's no way I'd miss this opportunity."

"Do you or those Indians have a gun?"

"I don't. Jack may have."

"Come into my office." He hurried toward a small building opposite the saloon. He handed her a pistol and a box of shells. "These men go crazy when they hear of a gold strike. Normally, not one of them would harm a white woman, but when the gold frenzy strikes them, they may do anything to get a claim. Be careful."

Within a few hours, Fortymile had emptied, except for Ogilvie, McPhee, and the Mounted Police. A ragtag flotilla of boats pushed off for Rabbit Creek, with Dinah and the two Indians in their midst.

Making infrequent stops, the three of them kept pace with the other gold seekers paddling furiously up the Yukon. More than once Dinah's heart went out to the two loyal Indians without any desire for gold who were willing to do this for her.

Dinah lost count of the hours before they reached the swampy shoreline where the Klondike emptied into the

Yukon. The mouth of the river must have been two hundred feet wide. Dozens of miners had set up tents along the Yukon and were fighting one another for claims.

"Not right place," Jack stated. "If strike is on Rabbit Creek, need to go up Klondike."

Jack paddled to the Indian village east of the Klondike. "Wait here," he said. "See if I can find help."

He returned soon with another Indian, whose unkempt condition contrasted sharply with the Crows'.

After listening to instructions from the newcomer, Jack said, "We leave the canoe here and walk to Rabbit Creek."

They tramped along the Klondike for a few miles before they came to Rabbit Creek. Miners thronged the area, driving stakes into the bank, but Jack motioned Dinah onward.

"Carmack found the gold many miles farther. Better to go on."

To forget her fatigue and how her feet ached, Dinah looked appreciatively at the little streams tumbling down the mountainside. The warm August sunlight bathed the hills in crimson, purple, and emerald green hues. Willows, cranberry, and salmonberry bushes lined the stream.

As she surveyed the scene of frenzied confusion, Dinah wondered where all these men could have come from. Their numbers convinced Dinah that she didn't have any time to lose. Shoving and pushing like the others, Dinah and the two Indians rushed up the creek. A few miles above the site of Carmack's discovery, they pounded stakes to mark three claims. Nannie and Jack disavowed any wish to look for gold, so Dinah staked claims for herself, her cousin Vance, and Seth.

At first she thought she should stake only one claim, but a grizzled old miner told her, "Once the government gets up here, they'll limit us to one, but there ain't no law on this creek yet. I'm marking a claim for my brother, and he lives in Seattle."

While they worked, Jack looked around in bewilderment. "Different creek. Think Rabbit Creek goes off that way." He waved in an easterly direction.

"Won't matter, Miss," the miner said. "If there's any gold here, this stream is as good as that other one."

Dinah decided the miner knew more about prospecting than she did. Besides, she was too tired to search further.

Knowing how much Vance would want to be in on the discovery, Dinah had no compunction about claiming for him, but how would Seth feel about her marking his claim? By the time they'd driven three-foot poles to mark the borders and she had skinned the bark off of three spruce trees and written on the date, August 22, 1896, along with their names, Dinah was too weary to care what Seth thought. She sprawled on the ground and immediately went to sleep.

Chapter Four

September 1896

*D*inah opened her eyes and quickly closed them again to shut out the bright sunlight shining directly on her face. The smell of food tantalized her, and she groaned as she struggled to a sitting position. Nannie had three fish steaming over a slow fire.

"How long have I slept?"

Nannie held up three fingers.

Three hours! I need three days.

"Where's Jack?"

Nannie motioned upstream. "Trying to catch more fish. Our supplies are almost gone."

"I was afraid of that, and there's no place to buy any, either."

"What do you do now?"

"Return to Fortymile to register these claims, and then I'm going to Circle. I hate to leave here that long, for someone might try to jump my claims, but I want to see if Dad has returned and get the supplies we have in the cabin. Will you and Jack go with me?"

"Yes, but then must go to fish camp and help family smoke food for winter. You come back here alone?"

"If I have to."

The valley where she'd staked the claims was about four hundred feet from rim rock to rim rock. The high hills on each side of the valley blocked her vision of the rugged mountains around them. Stunted spruce trees and high grass covered the hillsides.

The miner who'd given her instructions about staking her claims strode toward them, and Dinah held up a hand in greeting.

The man squatted beside her. "My name's Hank Sterling, ma'am. Wonder if I could buy one of the fish? I left most of my supplies at Fortymile."

"Give him my fish, Nannie," Dinah said. "And no pay wanted," she added, as the miner reached in his pocket.

After he'd eaten, Dinah asked Sterling to check her stakes.

"You've done a good job, Miss. I see you've staked a claim for Seth Morgan. Is he a friend of yours?"

"Why, yes! Do you know Seth?"

"I've seen him around here and there," Sterling said evasively. "Gold miners seem to congregate in one place."

Why was he so reluctant to say where he'd known Seth?

Sterling talked with an accent similar to Seth's. Had they known each other before they came to Alaska?

"What're your plans now, Miss?"

"I'm new at prospecting, but isn't the next move to file my claims? Ogilvie said I'd have to do that at Fortymile. I hate to leave this land unprotected, though."

"I'll watch out for your property. My pard left an hour ago for Fortymile to register our claims and bring our gear. I can't do any work until he returns. I'll patrol up and down the creek."

Noting that Hank wore a large holstered pistol and a rifle

slung across his back, Dinah decided he was capable of fighting off any claim jumpers. She and the two Indians took off as soon as Jack returned and reached Fortymile before the main horde of miners rushed to register claims.

Even though Ogilvie must have realized that Dinah was claiming for others, he didn't object. The three of them made short work of Fortymile and headed downstream.

"Where've you been?" Susie demanded when Dinah stepped into the cabin.

"Staking a gold claim."

"I'll bet. 'Honesty is the best policy.' Was the man your father?"

Dinah stared at her friend, unable to recall for a moment why she'd gone to Fortymile. So much had happened since she'd left Circle City three weeks ago.

"No. The man died before we got there, but I did see his body. There isn't any doubt in my mind that he wasn't Dad. Have you heard anything from him?"

"Not a word. He must have been wandering around without his glasses, fallen in a creek, and drowned, since all of his belongings were still in his camp. At least that's the way Waldo figures it. It's been close to three months. If he were alive, surely he would be back by now."

"I can't accept that, Susie. I have to keep on hoping. Is Seth in town?"

"Yes. He stopped by last night."

"I've got the most exciting news, and I want to tell him about it. There's a gold stampede upriver, and I staked a claim for him, as well as for myself."

Susie stared at Dinah. "Child, you're out of your mind."

"No, I'm not. I was at Fortymile when the news of the big strike came, and the Crows and I joined the general exodus from the town. As soon as I pack my clothes and gather supplies, I'm going back."

"You'll do nothing of the sort. Waldo has closed the

school, and we're heading back to Oregon before the freeze-up. You have to go with us. I can't leave you behind."

"Susie, you don't have any choice. I'm not leaving Alaska until I find my father, and besides, I've a good chance to make a fortune when that claim starts producing. Why don't you and Waldo go with me? If he hurries, he could even stake some land."

"Well, he won't do it, so that means I'm pulled two ways."

Dinah heard Susie muttering " 'Better an empty purse than an empty head' " as she left the Knight cabin to enter her own home.

She quickly surveyed their possessions, wondering what she could take with her. It would be impossible to carry any furnishings, but items from their well-stocked pantry would be her first priority. After packing those, she would decide what else to take.

A step at the door alerted her. *Seth!*

She flashed a welcome smile, but he frowned at her.

"Please tell me why you would strike out on a trip to Fortymile with only those two Indians for company?"

"Because you wouldn't go with me, that's why. I had to find out if that wounded man was my father."

"Was he?"

"No."

"All the more reason you should have stayed here. You had your trip for nothing."

"No, I didn't. Seth, the most exciting thing happened." She took his hand and pulled him to the bench behind the table. "While I was at Fortymile, George Carmack came in with the news that he had discovered gold on Rabbit Creek, a tributary of the Klondike River."

"George Carmack isn't noted for telling the truth."

"He was telling the truth this time. He had a can of gold that he'd gotten from the creek. So I rushed up the Yukon and staked some claims."

"You what?"

"Staked some claims—one for myself, one for you, one for my cousin Vance."

An angry wave passed across his face. "You did what?"

"Staked some claims," Dinah started to repeat, but he silenced her with a sweep of his hand.

"I heard you. I simply wondered why you had the nerve to stake a claim in my name. I have a gold mine."

"But not in Canada. I tell you, Seth, that country is underlaid with gold. It's the opportunity of a lifetime. Please go back with me. The Crows are going to fish camp, and I'd rather not go alone."

He stood up. "That's your problem. In the first place, I don't believe a word of it. Very little gold has been discovered in that area, and I'd just have the trip for my trouble. If you're wise, you'll go back to the States with the Knights."

He opened the door, and Dinah turned her back on him without answering. Her eyes glittered ominously. *He'll be sorry when I make a fortune and he's still grubbing in his ten-cent mine!*

Determined not to leave her malamutes behind, Dinah organized what food and clothing she could carry on her sled. She knew it wasn't good for the dogs to haul a heavy load in the summertime, but she had to have provisions. She lined a willow basket with an old blanket for Bathsheba to ride in, her worst suspicions having been confirmed. Bathsheba would soon become a mother, and she wondered what she could do with a family of kittens in a gold camp.

Still not giving up on her hope that her father was alive, Dinah wrote a note to leave for him.

The day before she left, Susie came to see her. "I've talked Waldo into going with you."

Dinah screamed and threw her arms around Susie's ample waist. "Oh, thank you, thank you."

"He still intends to leave before the freeze-up, but we can at least see you settled. He'll pole a canoe upstream."

"That will be fine. The dogs and I'll be traveling near the river, and we can camp together at night."

Dinah wrote a brief note to her cousin, Vance Miller, in San Francisco, and entrusted it to the mail carrier.

Dear Vance:
　Who says dreams never come true? Do you remember when we dreamed of finding gold? I've found enough for both of us. I've staked a claim for you beside mine near the Yukon River in Canadian territory. Come quickly; I think fortune is ready to smile on us.

Your cousin,
Dinah

Dinah stared in amazement at the spot where the Klondike and Yukon rivers merged. On the swampy north bank, along the foot of a steep, slide-scarred slope, a town had sprouted. The sound of a screeching saw forcing its way through spruce trees pierced the silence.

While Dinah waited for Waldo to maneuver his canoe to shore, she spoke to a grizzled miner standing nearby.

"What's happened? When I left here less than a month ago, there wasn't anything except a few poles marking claims."

"Joseph Ladue is what happened. He lived at Sixtymile, but when he heard about this strike, he packed up, lock, stock, and barrel, to move down here. Brought his sawmill, too. He got a land grant from the Canadian government and started this town."

"What's he named it?"

"Didn't make much difference to Ladue what it was called, but Ogilvie named the town site Dawson City after the chief of Canada's geographical survey, George Dawson. Ogilvie also set aside about twenty acres of land for use of the Mounted Police. I allow they'll be here most any day."

Numerous tents sprawled over the town site. Dinah's informant waved toward two buildings under construction.

"Ladue's building a warehouse and a saloon. He should be in business in a few days."

After she settled Susie and Waldo in a tent, Dinah searched out Ladue, a swarthy, brawny man of French Huguenot background who'd lived along the Yukon for fourteen years.

"What are your terms for buying lots?" she asked him.

"I have a one-hundred-seventy-eight-acre town site that I've staked into sixty-two-foot-wide streets and one-hundred-foot building lots. I'm selling them at five-hundred dollars each."

"Will you give me an option to buy two lots? I'll pay for them as soon as my claim starts producing."

"Your claim?"

"Yes, *my* claim. Don't you think a woman has a right to operate a mine?"

Ladue held up a pudgy hand. "Now, now! Do what you want to do, although I've always thought a woman should stay at home. That's why I left my sweetheart back east, and I'm going to marry her as soon as I strike it rich. I believe my chance will be here in Dawson City."

"Then you think there is gold?"

"I've seen the evidence already. Where'd you stake your claim, Miss?"

After Dinah explained the location as best she could, Ladue exclaimed, "Your not knowing the country may have been a lucky break for you. The Indian was right; you didn't stake on Rabbit Creek, which they're calling the Bonanza now. You're on Eldorado Creek, and the experts say it's richer than the Bonanza. Sure, I'll sell you some lots. Pick out the two you want."

Dinah walked around the town, finally choosing two lots on the third street from the river. She didn't know what she would do with them, but land would soon be scarce here, and she considered it a good investment.

The Knights and Dinah left Dawson City for the gold fields early the next morning. Dinah placed her dogs and most of their supplies in the care of a man who worked for Ladue until they could provide a place to store them. She carried Bathsheba's basket, and the cat purred contentedly.

A scow ferried them across the Klondike River. After they climbed a hill, the trail took them southeast until they came to a ridge road parallel to the Bonanza.

"In August," Dinah commented to Waldo, "I waded through brush and weeds to find my way. No such problem now."

"No, it appears that many miners have traveled this road."

Dinah looked behind them, where Susie struggled to keep up, and her conscience stirred that she'd asked this sacrifice of the older woman. "Doing all right, Susie?"

"I thought crossing the plains in forty-four was a hardship!" Susie panted. "But I was only sixteen then and many pounds lighter." She laughed merrily, adding, "I've missed those days during the years when life has been easier. I'm enjoying this, Dinah, and hope I can live to tell about it."

They reached Dinah's claim around seven o'clock. "I see no one has jumped our claims," she said, noting that the stakes hadn't been disturbed.

"Now what?" Waldo said as he looked over the barren area.

"We'll set up our tents for the time being so I can start to work the claim. But I must have a cabin and kennels before winter."

"I'll do the building for you. We'll have less than a month if we leave here before the freeze-up."

"I can probably hire someone to help with the building. Many men who staked claims don't have any money to buy mining supplies, so they'll be glad to work. I brought along what money Dad had, and that will take care of my needs until I find some gold."

To use her dad's money seemed tantamount to admitting

that he was gone for good, but when he came back, she'd repay him with gold from her mine.

"I'll need a cache to protect my supplies from the animals. It should be close to the cabin, for if food is scarce this winter, there may be some human predators."

"Dinah, I don't think I can go off and leave you here," Susie said while Waldo explored the area.

"I can't see any other way. I won't leave, and Waldo won't stay. You'll have to choose between us, and I think your place is with your husband."

Susie shook her head in exasperation. "I can't imagine where you got your stubborn ways. You're more like your great-uncle, Matt Miller, than your grandparents."

"That may not be so bad. Remember, he's the one who struck it rich," Dinah answered with a laugh.

"Is being rich that important to you? 'The love of money is the root of all evil.' "

"Susie, I believe a new age is dawning for women, and I want to pioneer in showing that women can achieve more than just being wives and mothers. I want to find gold to prove that I can do it, but after that, I'll use my riches to help others. I don't need a lot of gold for myself."

"That's not a proper attitude about marriage. You need to find a husband if you're going to stay here."

"Oh, do you have one in mind?" Dinah said flippantly, but she turned her head to prevent Susie from seeing the flush on her face. Feeling as she did about Seth would prevent her from taking an interest in any other man.

Hank wandered into their camp as the three of them ate their evening meal. Looking around, he said, "Morgan with you?"

"No, he isn't. These are my friends, the Knights."

"Struck any pay dirt yet?" Waldo asked.

"Yes, I found pay streak not more than two feet down, and I think you'll do the same, Miss," he said to Dinah.

"Lots more men here than when I left."

"Yes, there must be a hundred claims on the Bonanza and almost that many on the Eldorado."

"Doesn't seem like there's much chance for a man who comes in now," Waldo said, and Dinah wondered if he might be getting gold fever.

"But there is," Hank said. "Many miners staked claims and walked off and left them. A few got disgruntled because they didn't think the claims produced enough. Others didn't have the ten-dollar filing fee. Some left these areas and rushed over to other creeks. If you want a claim, I can point out several abandoned ones to you."

Waldo didn't comment, but Susie winked conspiratorially at Dinah behind his back.

"I intend to start digging tomorrow," Dinah said. "Could you give me a few pointers?"

Hank flexed his arms and fingers. "It's hard work, Miss, and you don't look like you're built for it, but I've seen scrawny little men outwork me many a day, so maybe you'll do all right." He picked up a shovel and lifted a chunk of dirt. "Right now, the top two or three feet of this ground is loose, and you can dig it without too much trouble. When you get down farther than that, you'll run into frozen muck where the ground has to be thawed by fire and shafts and tunnels built to bring out any gold that's there."

"That sounds like a great deal of work. I had visions of picking up gold like my uncle Matt did in California. He found a fortune just by pulling dead trees out of the ground. The gold nuggets had collected around the roots of trees."

"Yeah, I've heard stories like that, but taking gold from the ground in the north requires more effort than mining in the States."

"But some gold is found near the surface?"

"Yes, in some places, but us old miners think the most gold is at bedrock, which ranges ten to forty feet below the surface. This country may have once been covered with water, and the gold washed down into the crevices of the rock.

"To get *that* gold requires digging a shaft to the bedrock and removing the earth until you reach the rich gravel. At Fortymile we hauled pay dirt to the surface with a windlass. We dumped the dirt near the shaft, and when the water started running in the spring, we sifted the dirt and gravel to find the gold. I'll build a sluice box and show you how to use it to separate the gold particles from the sand."

Dinah could see her fortune slithering away before she even had it. She couldn't possibly do all of that digging. Perhaps sensing her dismay, Hank said, "If I were you, Miss, I'd hire some men to help with that heavy work. Many prospectors will move in here next summer without money, and since most of the claims are taken, they'll be glad to work for wages. In the meantime, you'll have no trouble digging on the surface, and you're likely to find plenty of gold there."

For the next two weeks, Susie and Waldo worked on the cabin, and when it neared completion, Waldo went into Dawson to buy a stove and a few cooking utensils from Ladue.

Dinah spent at least twelve hours daily groveling in the sand and gravel. She started with a tunnel ten feet long and five feet wide, and at first the digging was easy. As she poured the gravel into the sluice box, she peered anxiously to see if any gold showed up in the riffles after the water had washed the gravel away.

When she had dug about two feet into earth that grew harder the farther she dug, Dinah saw the first streaks of color in the gravel. She carefully scraped the black sand from the sluice box with a wooden paddle and placed it in a pan on the stove to dry. The next morning she used a magnet to draw off the black sand and found a layer of gleaming gold in the bottom of her pan.

When Hank came by to check her operations, he said, "You've got a good claim, Miss. I'd say this first pan will run thirty to forty dollars, which ain't bad, but you'll probably do better."

After Hank left, Dinah sat absentmindedly running her fingers through the fine gold particles.

"But is it worth it?" Susie asked. "Look at yourself," and she held a hand mirror in front of Dinah's face. " 'Fortune sometimes favors those she afterwards destroys.' "

Dinah closed her eyes at her image and pushed the mirror away. Dirt streaked her face, her hair hung dirty and lifeless, and dark circles ringed her eyes. She looked at her scratched, bleeding hands. Some blisters were open and running, others had become calloused. Her nails had worn to the edge of her fingers.

She didn't answer Susie, but the next morning, she picked up her shovel again, determined to work the ground she had claimed. A few hours later, she dipped up a scoop of dirt and uncovered a cache of gold. With trembling fingers, she reached into the crevice and found four large nuggets. Shaking her head to be sure she wasn't dreaming, she fondled the gold.

"Susie! Waldo!" she screamed. "Come and see."

Tears streaked Dinah's face when they reached her, and she thrust the nuggets toward them. Her throat was too tight for words.

"You've struck it rich!" Susie cried as Waldo took the nuggets and stared wonderingly at them.

"I've never seen so much gold in my life," he whispered.

Dinah scrambled to place the nuggets on the scales, and they weighed over a pound. At the price of gold now, that meant the four pieces were worth more than three hundred dollars.

Feeling rich as Croesus, she started digging furiously. She had apparently uncovered the same pay streak that Hank had found. She stared across the plots she'd marked for Seth and Vance. Since Hank's mine was beyond those, it seemed likely that their two claims were rich, too.

Stubborn man! Why couldn't Seth have come to the Klondike?

Waldo had never been a talkative man, but Dinah thought he seemed even quieter than usual that evening. About bedtime, he cleared his throat several times and blurted out, "Wife, I've been wondering about those abandoned claims. Do you think it might be a good idea for me to take one of them? That way we could stay here and keep an eye on Dinah."

Straight-faced, Susie said, "I think you'd better consider a little. Do you want to be stranded here this winter? Once the Yukon freezes, nobody will be going out. And we might run out of supplies."

When Waldo dropped his head, Susie flashed Dinah a wide smile and lifted her arm in a gesture of victory. Dinah knew that Susie was having the time of her life.

"But you do what you think best, Waldo. You know I don't want to leave Dinah alone."

Waldo spent the next day walking up and down the creek bank with Hank, and they finally settled on an abandoned claim about two miles upstream from Dinah's.

"I'll go into Dawson tomorrow to be sure no one else has filed on the claim, pay my fee, and start right in building a shelter."

"Can you file on a claim in Dawson now?" Susie asked.

"Hank says the Mounties have moved in and that claims can be filed in town."

"I'll go with you, Waldo, and bring back my dogs and the rest of our food supplies. I'll rest easier if they're here under our supervision. Are you going, Susie?"

"I wouldn't walk that eighteen miles again for any reason. I may never leave the Eldorado unless someone brings me a horse."

"I doubt there will be any horses here for a long time. Maybe we can harness a caribou for you to ride."

"You two go ahead, and I'll keep watch over things. If

Ladue has any food, you'd better buy some. Since we didn't expect to stay in the Klondike, I'm not sure that what we brought from Circle City will see us through the winter."

"I'll use my little horde of gold to buy food and make a payment on the land I bought from Ladue." She held up the first nugget she'd picked from the earth and caressed it lovingly. "I'll keep this for a souvenir to show my grandchildren."

"Better get a husband before you start counting your grandchildren," Susie said tartly.

As Dinah followed Waldo down the trail the next morning, she stared at the man's back and wondered about him. He purported to be as old as Susie, but Dinah had often doubted that. His heavy beard prevented close scrutiny of his face, but no wrinkles showed on his skin, and sometimes Dinah thought he probably wasn't as old as her father.

Thoughts of Nelson's disappearance banished the mystery of Waldo. Surely he wasn't dead, or his body would have been found. But why disappear in this manner?

Dinah smelled Dawson before she saw it, for the town had grown faster than sanitation facilities, and the stench rising from the area was stifling. Ladue's settlement consisted of tents, brush and pole shelters, and a few log cabins. On the slope above the town, several tents had been erected, and many people had settled on swampland across the Klondike.

Waldo and Dinah headed toward a small compound at the confluence of the Yukon and Klondike rivers where a British flag waved. Flies and mosquitoes buzzed around their heads. In spite of the littered, odorous streets, the town seemed orderly enough, for which the Mounties could no doubt be thanked. At the Mounted Police headquarters, the grounds were neat and clean.

"Miss Davis!" A pleasant voice hailed her, and Dinah turned to find Timothy McCormick at her elbow. "I've been wondering if I'd see you, now that I've been transferred to Dawson."

Dinah instantly wished she'd been more heedful of her clothing. Most of her better dresses had been left behind at Circle City, but she could have washed her hair. Still, she couldn't be rich and glamorous too, so she smiled up at Timothy as if she were properly groomed.

"How nice to see you, Timothy! It's good to know that the Mounties have landed."

"We haven't been able to do much yet, although we came as soon as we could. Until we have government officials to set up some rules, we can't keep these miners from fouling the rivers and the streets."

Timothy directed Waldo to the building where he could pay his filing fee, then led Dinah into his office. "Now tell me about yourself. Did you really stake out a claim?"

With a pert smile, Dinah answered, "Yes, I did, and I've found some gold, too." She took the canvas bag from her pocket and held it so he could peer inside.

"This is just the beginning. I believe I have a good claim, and I'm properly chaperoned. Waldo and his wife have been our friends for years, and they're with me."

"But what are you going to do with a lot of gold if you find it? Will you leave the north and go back to the States?"

"I honestly don't know. Until I learn something about my father, I don't want to leave. Have you heard whether he's returned to Circle City?"

"No, but then we haven't had any news from Circle. I'm concerned about you. Do you have enough food to last this winter? Many people are going to be hungry, for Ladue is quickly selling out of supplies. There's a boat leaving tomorrow. Maybe you'd better go on it."

Dinah shook her head. "I'm working my claim this winter. I wouldn't consider leaving. I have enough supplies."

Dinah accepted Timothy's invitation to dinner and to

spend the night inside their compound. Then she walked with Waldo to Ladue's and bought a few foodstuffs from the sparsely stocked shelves. She gave her gold as payment on the lots.

"A good thing you bought when you did, Miss. The price has risen considerably. You could sell the lots at a good profit, if you've a mind to."

When she left Ladue's warehouse, Dinah spotted Jack and Nannie Crow across the street.

"Jack, Nannie," she called, and they turned toward her.

"We came to look for you," Nannie said, with a slight smile in her slow way.

"Why?" Dinah asked quickly. "Do you have news of Dad?"

"No news," Jack answered. "We have finished the food supply for our village and thought you might need some help."

"Oh, I do. Perhaps you could shoot a caribou or moose for us. And I can use some baskets, Nannie."

"Dogs will need lots of meat for winter. We will catch fish and smoke it for them," Jack said. "But must go to our village before big cold."

"We'll start back to the claim in the morning. Where are you staying?"

Jack waved toward the Indian village across the river.

"Can you be here early? I want to take the dogs and the rest of our foodstuffs. I'll be glad of your help."

"We will do what we can," Nannie agreed. "You are our friend, and we think the Yukon winter will be too bad for you."

Dinah refused to let the words dishearten her. The presence of Jack and Nannie always buoyed her courage, and she resolved to survive the worst the Yukon sent her way.

Chapter Five

Winter 1896–97

*S*eth laid aside the letter and stared moodily into the fire. *Was something wrong at home?* The tone of his mother's letter differed from her usual cheery style, and she hadn't even mentioned Janice Sue. He picked up the letter and looked again at the last paragraph.

"Son, I appreciate the money you send so regularly, but I need you more than the money. Do you ever consider coming home? I remember you every day in my prayers, asking God to care for you and to restore the faith you once had. Surely you haven't forgotten the vows you took to preach the Word. Read Romans 10:14."

He didn't have to read the verse; he knew the words well enough: "How then shall they call on him in whom they have not believed? and how shall they believe in him of whom they have not heard? and how shall they hear without a preacher?"

Joseph Morgan had read those verses during his son's ordination service, but Seth had forced them from his mind for years. Seth realized that his father would have been displeased with his behavior over the past five years. His father would have much preferred that his son forget the murderer and honor the vow he'd taken to preach the gospel.

Seth left his cozy chair and paced the small room like a trapped animal. The snowstorm that had raged for days kept him from going to the mine on Birch Creek, and outside the walls of his cabin, Circle City offered Seth nothing in the way of entertainment.

Usually when he was in town, he visited with the Knights and Dinah, but they'd been gone four months now. He picked up a note he'd received from Dinah, written in September.

"Seth, it isn't any joke. This country is full of gold. So far I've been able to protect the claim that I made for you, but the more people who come, the more danger of claim jumpers."

He had read the note over and over, often wishing he'd gone to the Klondike before the freeze-up. The lure for gold had lost much of its pleasure for Seth, but he missed Dinah. Now that Nelson Davis had disappeared, he felt responsible for the girl. He should have gone with her.

A slight tap sounded on the door, and Seth admitted his friend, William Judge. Seth motioned the Jesuit priest into the easy chair he'd vacated. High cheekbones and huge, cavernous eyes emphasized by gold-rimmed spectacles gave Judge's face a skull-like quality. Seth served the priest a cup of coffee and a slice of canned plum pudding he'd bought at the trading post. Judge's emaciated body proved that he paid no attention to his diet. Snow crusted the man's footgear, and Seth laid a blanket at his feet.

"Slip off those wet moccasins, and I'll set them by the fire to dry. Wrap your feet in the blanket."

Silently, the priest did as he was bidden. Leaning back with a sigh, he said, "There's more news tonight from the Klondike. The town's citizens are becoming flustered."

"There's little doubt that gold has been found, but the quantity remains questionable."

"I expect a general exodus from Circle City before long. What do you expect to do in that event?" Judge asked, peering at Seth from behind his small glasses.

"I don't know. I'm worried about Dinah, and if there is an influx of prospectors to the area, I should go to look after her, now that her father is gone. And you?"

"If this town is vacated, I shall go to the Klondike. My ministry is with people, so I must be where they are."

"Let's hope they don't go before spring. A trip up the Yukon now would be too much for you," Seth replied, concern in his voice.

"God gives man the strength he needs for any task. Haven't you found that to be so, my friend?"

Seth laughed shortly. "If there is a God, and I doubt it, He won't give me any strength for the task I've set before me. You'll remember the Bible says, 'Vengeance is mine; I will repay, saith the Lord.' Well, I'm not pleased with God's timetable for vengeance; I'll take care of it."

If Seth had expected to shock the priest, he was doomed to be disappointed. Judge responded calmly, "You just think you'll take care of it, Seth. Perhaps you've turned your back on God, but He hasn't turned from you. You once dedicated your life to His service; God hasn't released you from that vow." He took a testament from his robe. "But this is no time to speak of vengeance. Tonight we celebrate the birth of the Prince of Peace."

Seth sat rigid and stared into the fireplace when the priest started reading, " 'And it came to pass in those days, that there went out a decree from Caesar Augustus, that all the world should be taxed,' " ending with, " 'Behold, I bring you good tidings of great joy, which shall be to all people. For unto you is born this day in the city of David a Saviour, which is Christ the Lord.' " The priest knelt to pray, and against his will, Seth found himself on his knees.

But he didn't pray. He tried to communicate with God about his mother, Janice Sue, and Nelson Davis, but there seemed to be a blank wall between him and God. He trembled at the thought that God might no longer be concerned with Seth Morgan.

Seth helped the priest stand, at the end of his prayer, and clasped his hand. Leaving the cabin, Judge said, "I pray that the peace of God will find its way into your heart, my friend."

Two weeks later, Seth sat in Henry Ash's saloon, not for a drink, but simply for human companionship, when the door opened to admit Arthur Walden, a Yukon dog driver. He carried a packet of letters from the Klondike, and although Walden asked for something warm to drink, Ash ignored him to sort through the mail. Finding the letter he wanted, Ash shoved the rest of the mail aside.

Seth walked to the bar to see if he had another letter from Dinah, and he was turning away empty-handed when Ash shouted, "Help yourself to the whole shooting match, boys. I'm off to the Klondike."

Ash leaped over the bar and headed outside. The miners whooped and rushed for the liquor behind the bar, but Seth pushed them out of his way. He picked up the letter the bartender had tossed aside. The message from one of Ash's friends in Dawson confirmed the abundance of gold in the Klondike.

Thoughtfully, Seth left the orgy behind him and walked toward the little mission where William Judge lived.

"It's started," he said when the priest opened the door.

"I know. I've already had two men trying to buy my sled dog. One of them offered me a thousand dollars for it. I bought the dog two years ago for twenty-five dollars."

"What are you going to do?"

"Pack what I can haul on my sled and head up the Yukon."
"The temperature is thirty below." When the priest didn't
answer, Seth said, "If you'll wait two days, I'll go with you."

As he walked to his cabin, Seth wondered at his sudden
decision to go to the Klondike. He made a good living at the
mine on Birch Creek. Why forsake it for a risky venture? But
he didn't think the priest should be traveling alone in his
undernourished condition. Then, too, there was his concern
for Dinah. How was she standing the bad weather? He didn't
blame her for not writing, since he hadn't answered the other
letter. Had she found that she didn't need his help anymore?

The next morning, Seth started his preparations for leaving Circle City. By the time he packed all of his foodstuffs
and warmest clothing on his sled, there was little room left
for books. He shoved aside the Bible his mother had forced
upon him before he left South Carolina, choosing instead the
works of Walt Whitman, John Greenleaf Whittier, and two
volumes by Jules Verne.

Seth boarded up the windows of his cabin and padlocked
the door, hoping that no one would bother the possessions
he must leave behind. His preparations completed, he
paused indecisively in the blowing snow, unlocked the door,
retrieved the Bible, and put it in his pocket.

The town's citizens straggled out on the frozen Yukon in
twos and threes. Those with dog teams raced away over the
ridges of ice, soon to be swallowed up in the drifting snow.
Determined not to leave William Judge behind, Seth slowed
his pace to that of the priest, who harnessed himself with his
single dog to spare the animal. Seth's two huskies protested
at the slow pace, but Seth stayed beside the priest, and in
their twenty days of travel, he fed the man from his own
provisions, knowing that Judge's sled was loaded with more
medicine than food.

Although the toilsome journey galled Seth, the priest
never complained. His body resembled a walking skeleton,

but his eyes gleamed with a vision of the hospital he hoped to build in Dawson. Seth wondered if Judge's first view of the new Yukon town dampened his enthusiasm: Dawson consisted of a half-dozen houses and scores of dirty tents scattered haphazardly over the frozen swamp land.

Seth couldn't imagine why anyone would build a town in such an unpromising spot, but it was close to the gold fields, and he reasoned that men would live anyplace if money could be made by dwelling there. Seth rested two days before he headed up the Bonanza trail to see Dinah.

For two months Dinah worked her claim in shadowy darkness. At midday, the darkness lightened to a few hours of dim twilight. When the creek froze solidly and she couldn't separate gold dust from gravel in the sluice box, she piled the dirt into a dump to await the spring thaw.

When the temperature dropped to fifty below zero, Susie absolutely refused to let Dinah work on the claim. For days the three of them existed in the murky cabin that was lighted by a few candles. The ceiling and walls of the cabin glistened with ice, which melted from the heat of the stove to form icicles. Food two feet from the stove froze in minutes.

Dinah prowled the room like a caged tiger. Waldo lay on his bunk and stared at the ceiling, while Susie talked incessantly, even though the others wouldn't answer her. Only Bathsheba seemed content as she played with her three kittens in a warm box near the stove.

"Susie," Dinah said, "I've about gotten all of the easy gold I can on this claim. And even that hasn't been easy when you consider how I've had to keep a fire going most of the time to thaw the ground. Won't spring ever come?"

"Getting cabin fever, are you?"

"Oh, it isn't that so much, but I'm tired of guarding everything I have. Not the gold—at this point, nobody cares much about gold. But it's terrible to have to watch my dogs to keep them from being killed for food."

"People resent it because you have food for the dogs when they don't have enough."

"We've shared what we have—you know that. I think it's foolish to kill our dogs when we may need them."

"According to Hank, things aren't as bad here as in Dawson. It's a miserable place. There are only two hens in town, and people stand around waiting for them to lay eggs that they snatch up for a dollar each. The only place anyone can take a bath is in a wooden laundry tub in a heated tent. Costs a dollar and a half for five minutes in the tub, and they all have to bathe in the same water."

"I've gotten to the place I don't even mind being dirty, but I do miss not having any news of the outside world. No news at all since October," Dinah complained.

"Dawson citizens are reduced to reading labels on packing boxes for entertainment. People are crazy to endure such conditions for gold," Waldo contributed, "the three of us included."

"Well, it's near the middle of February by my calculations," Dinah said. "Winter should let up soon. I can tell there are more daylight hours every week. I'm hoping to lease my mine to some newcomer who came too late to get a claim of his own. I have more gold now than I've ever dreamed of having, but sometimes I'm tempted to dig into those claims I made for Vance and Seth."

"Somebody will take the claims if they don't hurry up."

"If I know Vance, he's on his way now, but of course he can't arrive until the spring thaw."

"If you're going to give someone a lay on your claim, what do you intend to do? Go back to Oregon?" Susie questioned.

"Not to stay, but I will have to go out with my gold. It won't do me much good in its present state. Then I'm thinking about building a hotel in Dawson. Considering the deplorable living conditions in the town, I believe a good hotel would be welcomed."

"And once news of this gold rush gets outside, there'll be a stampede toward the Klondike."

Dinah still brooded on the vile weather two days later when a knock sounded on the door and Susie called, "Come in."

Dinah stared as Seth's tall figure filled the doorway, then ran to him and threw her arms around his waist.

"Seth, you came at last!"

"I didn't have much choice," he said testily, hating himself for being short with her. "It was either come to the Klondike or stay in Circle alone. Everyone else headed this way."

"It's time you came," Susie said. "Your claim is still lying untouched, but Dinah and Waldo have had a dickens of a time keeping claim jumpers off of it."

"And the gold here is unbelievable. Look," Dinah said as she raced around the room showing him the gold dust she'd stored in cans, jars, and canvas bags. "You'd never find so much wealth in that claim on Birch Creek."

Seth's face mirrored astonishment. "Then all the reports are true?"

"Yes. I've got a big dump of dirt to wash out as soon as the creeks start flowing."

"Sit down, Seth," Susie invited. "We're just ready to eat. This caribou steak is pretty good."

When Seth took a newspaper from his pocket, Dinah pounced on it with delight.

"The mail carrier brought that to Circle City just a few days before I left."

"Tell me what you read," Susie said as Dinah scanned the first page. "No news is good news, I've always heard, but I'm eager for some news, good or bad."

"Queen Victoria is ill, and so is Pope Leo. War is threatening between England and Russia, and a fight is being promoted between James J. Corbett and Bob Fitzsimmons," Dinah read.

"Where's Waldo?" Seth asked after they'd finished their meal.

"He's taken a claim upcreek a few miles, and he stays there some of the time. You can live with him until you get established." Reaching for her heavy mackinaw, Dinah continued, "Come on, Seth. I'll show you around."

"I traveled over two hundred miles up the Yukon without a guide," Seth replied testily. "I think I can find my way along Eldorado Creek."

"Oh, don't be such a grouch," Dinah said. "Someone might shoot you for a claim jumper if I'm not along. Everybody knows me."

"I'll bet they do. But I hardly knew you. You look like a skeleton. A dirty one, at that."

Dinah refused to start quarreling with Seth. She motioned to him to follow her.

In spite of Seth's protests, Dinah worked beside him when he started his claim. "I have all the gold I can store right now, and I want to see if you have a rich pay streak."

"But I want you to be a lady. Have you looked at yourself lately? Your face resembles a piece of leather, your hands are calloused, and your hair doesn't look like it's been combed for weeks. Gold mining isn't any job for a woman."

"I haven't done so badly," she replied tartly. "But I'll admit that I've had enough of this, and I'm going to settle down to more genteel living. I've decided to use my gold to build a hotel in Dawson."

"A hotel! You're going from bad to worse. Take your gold back to Oregon and stay there."

"And miss all this excitement? Dawson will soon be the greatest place in the world. Even if I didn't want to know what had happened to Dad, I wouldn't leave. If you strike it rich, are you going to leave?"

"Not until I'm convinced that my father's murderer isn't in the North."

"Then you haven't heard anything more about the gun and the watch?"

"Not a clue as to how they happened to be here."

"What do you intend to do if you find your father's murderer?"

He glared ominously at the frozen ground. "I don't know."

By alternately thawing the ground and shoveling, it took them more than a week to dig through the two feet of gravel. But the same pay streak that ran through Dinah's claim was found in Seth's, and in six weeks they had accumulated a large amount of gold dust.

"Now what?" Susie said when Dinah, Seth, and Waldo tried to figure how much their gold would be worth in the States. "You've got the gold. Now what are you going to do with it?"

"I'm going to build a hotel in Dawson on those two lots I bought from Ladue, but I'll have to go home to order the furniture and fixtures."

"I want to send my mother and Janice Sue some of my riches, and I'll have to go somewhere to do that. I don't care what I do with the rest of it," Seth said.

"If the two of you want to go Outside, Susie and I can watch all of the claims," Waldo volunteered. "In return, you can take our gold with you."

"I'll go, because I know Dinah will, and woman or not, I don't think it's safe for her to travel alone with so much gold."

"You're right, I am going, with or without you, but I'd rather have your company."

"Thanks," Seth responded dryly.

"But I want to leave now, and I heard in Dawson last week that the first boat may not arrive until late May or

June, depending on the thaw. If we wait that long, we won't reach the States in time to come back here this summer."

"What other choice do you have?" Waldo asked.

"Go over the ice by dogsled to Alaska's coast and catch a steamer to Portland."

Waldo stared at her in amazement. "But that would be a terrible trip. What route would you take?"

"Ladue says that some people have traveled along the Yukon to Fort Selkirk, then cut across country either on the Dalton Trail or on a route through White Pass."

"How long would that take?" Seth asked.

"If we're lucky, we could be in Portland in a month," Dinah answered.

" 'We make our own luck,' " Susie said.

"We can take the dogs to haul the gold. Seth and I can both handle a team, and Jack can go along to bring back the animals after we reach the coast. I'm not going to sell Shadrach, Meshach, and Abednego. They're family."

"It's a crazy idea," Seth said, "but if you're foolish enough to try it, I'm foolish enough to go with you."

The next day, Dinah and Seth went on snowshoes to the winter village of the Crows, about ten miles downriver from Dawson. Jack agreed to go with them, but he said, "No time to waste. If a thaw sets in, I'd not have time to return. Could be an early spring."

"I figure it's about the first of April, and if we leave tomorrow, you should be back by mid-May," Seth said. "The return trip would be faster because you wouldn't have the gold. We'll sell one sled, and you can hitch all five dogs together."

The temperature hovered at twenty below zero the next morning. The gold loaded the sleds more heavily than they would have liked, but the three malamutes and Seth's huskies hadn't worked much all winter, and they'd been fed well.

"Dogs will do all right," Jack said, "if we carry provisions on our backs."

"Don't bother with many changes of clothing," Seth told Dinah. "We'll take one tent for the three of us, and as much food as we can carry."

"Let's have a prayer before you set out," Waldo said, and he knelt beside the table, committing them and their journey to God's protection. When Waldo finished, Dinah looked quickly at Seth, who stared out the window with unbowed head.

In Dawson, Dinah looked up Ladue to give him instructions about the hotel he'd agreed to build for her.

"I want a three-story building. Make the first floor of logs at least three feet off the ground. Building so close to the Yukon leaves us liable to flooding."

"That's a good idea, Miss," Ladue agreed. "When your lots are only three blocks from the river, you could see some water."

"The upper floors can be frame. I'll have a restaurant on the first floor, sleeping rooms on the second and third. Build my own quarters and the kitchen in an ell connected to the main construction."

"You seem to have your plans well made," Ladue said, admiration in his voice.

"That's all I had to think about during the cold days when I couldn't work outside. We intend to return about the first of July. Will you have the hotel finished by then?"

"I'll try, Miss."

For six days they followed the frozen Yukon until they reached Fort Selkirk at the junction of the Lewis and Pelley rivers, where the Yukon began. The temperature stayed below zero even during the daylight hours. Running to keep pace with the spirited dogs was more strenuous than Dinah had imagined, and when they stopped for the night, she was so tired, she wouldn't have eaten if Seth hadn't made her. They slept warmly enough because they crowded the five dogs into the tent with them. By morning, Dinah always felt rested and looked forward to the day's journey.

At Fort Selkirk, they spent the night inside the building and tied the dogs in the trader's kennels. As they prepared to leave the fort, the trader inquired, "Are you going along water all the way?"

"No, we intend to follow the Dalton Trail. That's three hundred and fifty miles, but we thought we wouldn't run into soft ice on that route," Seth said.

"That's a good way," the trader encouraged them. "Dalton has made several trips on it this winter, and many people have gone out that way. Let me give you a map of a few places where you'll find cabins and food caches. The Mounties have worked all winter to keep supplies available for stampeders. You'll reach the Chilkat Indian village beside Lynn Canal, and from there, it's only a short distance to Skagway, a new town that's sprung up. Steamers leave there for the States."

As they climbed higher into the mountains, the temperatures plummeted at night and blinding snowstorms often obliterated the trail. However, they must have met more than twenty-five stampeders heading for Dawson during the first week.

"I can't believe this," Dinah said. "All these people braving the wilderness for gold they'll never find."

Seth laughed. "You're a good one to talk. *We're* out here when we could both be snug in a log cabin back on the Eldorado. And why? Because you wanted to take out our gold and head back into the madhouse as quickly as possible."

"I guess you're right," Dinah admitted meekly. "But those

people aren't going to find any gold. All of the good streams are staked now."

"We know that, but they don't. Nor would they believe us if we told them. So let them dream."

During the days of travel, Dinah nurtured some dreams of her own. She and Seth enjoyed the same companionship they'd shared during the week they'd traveled to the Indian potlatch last summer. She had even dared to hope that their days together might foster a romantic tendency from Seth, but he continued to treat her as a sister.

As she often had before, she wondered why Seth didn't show any interest in women—at least none she'd ever noticed. Had he left a sweetheart in South Carolina? Sometimes she even questioned if the Janice Sue he harped on was really his sister. Perhaps she was a friend he intended to marry someday.

Once she asked, "Seth, you do intend to go back to the Klondike, don't you?"

He looked at her, amazement on his face. "Certainly. Do you think I'd let you undertake that trip alone?"

Her face flamed, and she said, "I just wondered."

"You'd be better off to spend your time wondering about how we're going to make it to Lynn Canal. We still have several days of rough travel," he said crossly, and Dinah's hopes of romance slithered away.

Chapter Six

May 1897

*T*he steamer chugged slowly into Portland Harbor, and Dinah excitedly pointed out landmarks to Seth. Although eager to set foot in her home again, Dinah stayed by their cargo until Seth hired a carriage to take them to the smelting works. When they piled their considerable horde of gold on the counter, the clerks stared in amazement, but Seth and Dinah evaded all questions about the origin of their gold.

"We arrived from Alaska today," Seth said. "That's all we intend to say right now."

"Betcha this came from the Klondike," one of the clerks said, and a disgusted look crossed Seth's face. They had hoped to escape any special attention.

Clerks weighed their nuggets and dust, figured the gold's worth in dollars, and gave them certificates of credit at one of Portland's banks. The raw gold itself would be refined and shipped to the United States mint in San Francisco, there to be converted into coins.

Dinah's share of the gold netted $125,000; Seth's share was $75,000; and for Waldo and Susie, the total came to $60,000.

As they left the smelting works, overawed by their fortunes, Seth said, "What now?"

"After we deposit these certificates in a bank, I want to check into a hotel and soak in a tub for hours. I'll need to buy some new clothes and improve my personal appearance before my grandmother sees me. She might faint if she saw me the way I look now."

"When do you plan to start north again?"

"After a short visit with my grandparents near Oregon City, I intend to buy my hotel fixtures in Seattle and have them shipped from there. What are you going to do?"

"As soon as I send some money to South Carolina, I'm ready to return. But I'll wait for you."

"There's no need to. Probably you should go back as soon as possible to help Susie and Waldo," Dinah said, though in her heart she wanted him to stay.

"There *is* a need to," Seth said testily. "The Chilkoot Trail is no place for a woman alone."

"Then if you're intending to force your company upon me, come and meet my grandparents. I hope they have word from Vance. If he doesn't reach the Klondike this summer, that claim of his may be taken away, and I don't want anyone else working between our mines."

"I'll go with you. Will you be ready tomorrow?"

"No, I'll need at least two days to obtain a suitable wardrobe."

After they'd deposited their gold certificates in a bank, Seth and Dinah checked in at a second-rate hotel. Seth wanted to remain as inconspicuous as possible with their wealth, so Dinah chose lodgings where she hadn't stayed with her grandparents.

"Do you want me to take you to the dressmaker's?"

"Of course not. I can find my way around Portland. I've been here many times."

"Then I'll meet you at six o'clock for dinner," Seth said as Dinah entered the room across the hall from his.

The hotel manager soon sent up the hot water that Dinah had requested. She scrubbed and soaked in the tub for over an hour, looking in dismay at her rough hands and her muscular arms and legs. There wasn't an ounce of spare flesh on her slender body, and her ribs showed prominently through the skin.

"And he expects me to be ladylike! How can I, when I'll never look like one again?" Dinah moaned aloud.

Dinah washed her hair and, after it dried somewhat, she piled it around her head. Donning her only clean undergarments and wearing a dress she'd taken north to Alaska two years ago, she sallied out, hoping she wouldn't excite too much attention before she bought some new clothes.

A huge woman, swathed in a black gown, favored Dinah with a skeptical smile and uplifted eyebrows when she entered the shop. Dinah took a roll of bills from her reticule and waved them before the woman, whose slight smile broadened into a wide grin.

"And what can I do for you, Miss?" she inquired graciously.

"I need a complete wardrobe, including underclothes. I want at least one dress to take with me today and two or three garments to be ready tomorrow. You can have a week to make the remainder. I'd also like to have your maid do something with my skin and hair."

The woman lifted the tangled split strands of Dinah's hair and clucked nervously. She examined Dinah's hands, with their broken nails, calluses, and scratches.

"You're a challenge to me, Miss. Where have you been?"

"In the Klondike."

"Oh," the woman replied, obviously never having heard of the gold region.

The hairdresser took two hours, but when she finished,

Dinah smiled at her transformation in the mirror. The woman had used oils and shampoo to restore Dinah's hair to its original blond luster. With the help of heated curling tongs, soft curls had been arranged around her forehead and the rest of her hair gathered into a cluster of curls at the nape of her neck.

But no amount of oils and creams could restore her skin to the condition it had been before she'd toiled for months in the harsh Klondike winter. Her weather-beaten skin was a shade darker than before, but she took pleasure in the reflection she viewed in the mirror.

The woman's supply of dresses was broader than Dinah had expected, and she ordered a two-piece traveling suit of navy broadcloth, two cotton dresses, and a dinner dress. The latter, made of pink satin, fit snugly at waist and hips, but the gored skirt increased to a wide hemline. Leg-of-mutton sleeves narrowed from the wrist to well above the elbow and expanded into soft folded puffs. A large white lace flounce extended from neck to shoulders.

Dinah purchased a black wool cape with a small upstanding collar. As she started to leave with her purchases, she noticed a poster advertising some rather unusual garments.

"What are these?" she asked the proprietor.

"Bloomers, Miss Davis. They are becoming popular for cyclists in the East and with women who do a great deal of walking."

The two women pictured wore voluminous trousers buttoned securely below the knee. Black stockings and low shoes completed the costume. Instantly Dinah realized how helpful such garments would be in scaling the Chilkoot, but she hesitated momentarily. How would Seth react to these costumes?

The hesitation didn't last long. Seth Morgan had no control over her actions, so with a mischievous smile, she said,

"I'd like two sets of those. Make the bloomers of wool and the blouses of another heavy fabric."

Dinah wore a new cotton dress when she met Seth for dinner. He gave her an appraising glance and smiled. "That's more like it. I'd forgotten that you were a pretty girl."

Coloring slightly, Dinah said, "I see you've spent some of your hard-earned gold on clothing, too," for Seth had appeared in a new brown suit, white shirt, and tie.

"These are the first dress garments I've bought since I left South Carolina seven years ago."

Taking Dinah's arm, Seth guided her toward the dining room. The waiter looked at Dinah in surprise when she placed her order. "I want three fried eggs, servings of all the fresh vegetables you have, and a quart of milk."

"I'll take the same, except add a quart of lemonade and a can of pineapple to my order."

The waiter was obviously puzzled at their choices, but he soon placed the food before them. They talked very little while they consumed the fresh food they hadn't enjoyed for months.

Seth ordered a cup of coffee, and while he drank it slowly, Dinah said, "I don't know what to tell my grandparents about Dad. That's really going to be a blow to them."

"Just tell them the truth. There isn't anything else you can do."

"But what is the truth? Do you think there's any possibility he's still alive?"

"No, I don't. He's been gone almost a year now."

Tears stung Dinah's eyelids. "I can't give him up."

"It seems both of us are destined to sorrow over our fathers," Seth said, and at the tone of his voice, Dinah blinked away her tears.

"I'm sorry, Seth. I'm not very thoughtful at times. At least I still have hope that Dad might be alive, but you know you won't have your father again."

"It wouldn't be so difficult if I could escape from the memory of his death, but it follows me everywhere I go. I've been elated today to finally have enough money to provide for Mother and Janice Sue. But when I left the bank after making arrangements for the transfer of funds to South Carolina, I met Sam."

"I don't know. . . ," Dinah started.

Seth interrupted, "I told you about Sam—he's the son of the ex-slave whom my father befriended."

"Oh, yes, I remember now. He saw the man who killed your father."

Seth nodded. "And *his*. We came to Colorado together, but when I left Cripple Creek to go to Alaska, Sam decided to stay behind. He had no liking for any colder weather than we had there."

The waiter came with their checks, and when Dinah would have paid for her own meal, Seth said, "Allow me. I'm feeling magnanimous tonight."

They moved into the lobby, and Seth indicated two chairs in a secluded alcove.

"Let's sit here, and I'll finish telling you about Sam. He heard that the man who killed our fathers had moved to Oregon, and he came here to see for himself. He's been roaming around for three months, and he's heard nothing to give him a clue to the man's identity."

"I suppose you told him about the items you've found in Alaska?"

"Yes, and he's agreed to come north to help me find the man. He won't go with us, but I gave him enough money to take a steamer."

"Are you suspicious of anyone in particular?"

"I've eyed every man I've seen for months, and I don't have a suspect. Among the hundreds in the Klondike, it would be hard to pick out one."

"I've often wondered about Hank Sterling. He seems to

avoid you, and he knew who you were when I staked the claim. But I hope it isn't him. He's been so good to me."

Seth absentmindedly caressed Dinah's glowing hair, and she thrilled at his touch, but his mind was still on the past.

"I suppose it will be the last person we'd suspect. I only hope that Sam will know, and I can settle this dilemma once and for all."

"I'll ask you the same question I did months ago. What will you do if you do find your father's murderer? Don't you think it's time to forget this foolish vengeance?"

"It isn't foolish," Seth retorted. "I can imagine your reaction if you should learn that someone had killed your father. But even when I try to forget the cause of his death, something always occurs to make me remember—like meeting Sam today."

Dinah reached for his hand. "I am sympathetic about your problem, Seth, but I dislike having you pursue a course that could destroy you as well as your father's assassin."

He lightly squeezed her fingers. "After Sam spends some time in the Klondike, if he doesn't ferret out anyone, perhaps I can forget it. Sorrow and vengeance make poor companions."

After their first few months in Alaska, Dinah hadn't experienced any longing for home, but her heartbeat accelerated and tears filled her eyes when their rented carriage rounded a bend in the road and her grandparents' home spread before her. The two-story frame house had been built around the original log cabin that Becky and Maurie had lived in at first.

A lithe man with straight gray hair touching his shoulders rose from a chair on the broad porch when Seth stopped the carriage.

Dinah waved and shouted, "Grandpa," and Maurie Davis vaulted down the steps to greet her. Maurie lifted her from the seat and enveloped her in a bear hug, shouting, "Becky, come quick!"

Becky appeared at the door of the house and uttered a glad cry. Seth was forgotten in the joyous homecoming. He carried their luggage to the porch and drove the carriage toward the barn.

"Let me look at you," Dinah cried as she stood back from her grandparents. Maurie Davis, at eighty-five, still displayed the strength and vigor he'd possessed fifty years ago when he'd guided a wagon train across the Oregon Trail. Dinah noted a slight stoop to Grandmother Becky's shoulders and wrinkles marred her fair skin, although she retained the beauty that had won her husband.

"But where's Nelson?" Becky said, looking around as if the homecoming wasn't quite complete.

"Oh, Grandma, I hate to tell you," Dinah started, and tears flooded her eyes as she threw herself again into Becky's arms. "He disappeared months ago, and we don't know what's happened to him."

"Why didn't you come home at once? And where are Susie and Waldo?" Maurie demanded. He looked suspiciously at Seth, who approached the house. "Who's that?"

"There's so much to tell you. Can't we go inside? But first let me introduce you to Seth Morgan. He's a friend of Dad's—and of mine, too, I guess," she finished, with a slight smile.

Maurie shook hands with Seth, and when they started to enter the house, Dinah bumped into a slender, dark-headed youth.

"What's going on?" the youth demanded. Then he looked at Dinah, and their recognition was simultaneous.

"Dinah!"

"Cousin Vance!"

They grabbed hands and swirled around the porch as if they were still the children who'd had so much in common.

"What are you doing here? You should be guarding my gold mine. Don't tell me that was all a joke and you got me excited for nothing!"

"So you did receive my letter. It's no joke! Your claim is waiting for you, and Waldo and Susie are guarding it. We have to leave here soon to make it back to the Klondike before winter sets in."

"What claim? Go back to the Klondike? Have you two lost your minds?" Maurie demanded.

"Haven't you told them?" Dinah said to Vance.

"I only arrived yesterday evening, and since it was pretty obvious that they hadn't heard about your adventure, I didn't mention the letter you'd sent me."

With a sigh, Dinah said, "Let's sit down then, because it's a long story." Seated in a rocking chair with her grandparents on the couch opposite her, Dinah explained. "We had written you that the Indians hadn't responded well to the school Dad and Waldo established, and both of them became discouraged. So Dad took a notion to go prospecting. He hasn't been heard of since. I've searched everywhere I could, and the Mounties have been on the lookout for him. I should have written you, but I kept thinking that he'd be found."

Maurie blew his nose and put his arm around Becky, who wept silently. "But that makes no sense. Seems there would be some trace of him."

"Alaska and the Yukon Territory are vast regions, sir," Seth said. "Many things could have happened to him. Remember there are grizzlies, as well as other ferocious bears. He could have drowned in one of the treacherous streams, and I, personally, think that's what happened."

"Isn't there a chance he could be a prisoner of the natives?" Maurie asked.

"A chance, perhaps, but quite unlikely. For one thing, the Indians aren't hostile to whites, and we have good friends among the tribes. If there was a white man being held prisoner, we'd have heard it," Seth answered.

"That's right," Dinah added. "Two of my best friends are Athapaskans, and they helped me hunt for Dad. It was while we were out searching for him that I heard of a gold strike on the Klondike River, a tributary of the Yukon. Actually, the gold had been found on a stream called Rabbit Creek, but it's named the Bonanza now."

"We know about the Klondike. News has filtered into the States about it all winter. You mean you've been there?" Maurie demanded.

"Since last September. I went in with the first wave of stampeders," Dinah hurriedly said. Perhaps news of the gold rush would take her grandparents' thoughts away from Nelson for the time being.

Dinah had to smile at the eagerness on Vance's face and the consternation displayed by her grandparents. "I wasn't far away from the area where gold was discovered, so I joined the rush and staked out three claims: one for myself, one for Vance, one for Seth."

"A claim for yourself," Becky exclaimed. "But, Dinah, you're a lady!"

Dinah threw Seth an angry look when he cleared his throat.

"I'm also a rich gold miner."

"Then there really *is* gold there?" Vance breathed.

Taking the certificate of credit from her reticule, Dinah said, "I worked all winter, and with my own two hands, I found gold worth one hundred and twenty-five thousand dollars. The experts think that at bedrock, the riches will be even greater."

Maurie reached for the certificate Dinah held out to him. He shook his head. "I can't believe this could happen twice in one family. Your grandfather, Vance, and now Dinah. There must be a curse on us."

"It didn't seem to hurt Gramps. He's still levelheaded," Vance disagreed.

"And I hope you'll be the same, Dinah," Becky said. "What do you intend to do with all this money?"

"Basically the same thing Uncle Matt did. Not that I'll start a steamboat industry, but I'm having a hotel built near the gold fields, and I'm going back this summer to operate it. I've had enough groveling in the dirt. Seth says he'll take a lease on my claim."

Becky shook her head wonderingly. "I can't believe it, Dinah. You were only a child when you left here; you returned a wealthy businesswoman."

"How did you manage to get here so early in the season?" Maurie asked Seth. "Aren't the rivers in Alaska still frozen?"

"We came by dogsled to Skagway, then took a ship to Portland. Summer is short in the Klondike, and we have to start back next week to be sure we reach our claims before winter."

"Are we returning by boat?"

"No, my boy," Dinah told Vance with a laugh. "We're going over the Chilkoot Trail."

"Never heard of it," Vance said.

"So much the better, then. You won't know what to expect," Seth commented with a smile.

"What's the name of this town that's sprung up?" Maurie asked. "Does it amount to much?"

"Dawson City. There are only a few buildings now, but it will boom before this year's out," Seth responded.

Shaking his head, Maurie said, "And it will be worse than the California gold rush, too, and that was horrible. You'd better stay home, Dinah. I don't want you up there alone if Dawson becomes anything like San Francisco in its heyday."

"I won't be alone. Susie and Waldo are there, and Vance can keep me company now. Besides, Seth keeps his eye on me."

She smiled saucily at Seth, and he frowned in her direction.

"I read the news when we were in Portland, and I'd say this gold strike will cause a general exodus from the States," Seth suggested.

"Yes, especially here in the Northwest, where there's been a depression since the panic of eighteen ninety-three," Maurie agreed. "Men will see this gold strike as a cure-all for their troubles."

"Bryan's prophecy that the country would be crucified on a cross of gold has come true," Vance said. "Gramps believes that Americans have hoarded gold until it's almost out of circulation."

"Besides that, the world is at peace now, and the Klondike will have no rival for public attention," Maurie continued. "The newspapers will have a heyday."

"I guess the war between Russia and England didn't materialize," Seth commented.

"That's true," Maurie agreed. "And Queen Victoria and the pope recovered, and Fitzsimmons won his prize fight with Jim Corbett."

Seth laughed. "So the newspapers won't have any other subject except the Klondike."

Becky stood and motioned to Dinah. "Come help me prepare the meal. We'll enjoy woman talk, not politics."

But in the kitchen, she sat at the table and started crying. "Now tell me about your father," she finally asked. "What do you think happened to him? Is there any chance he's still living?"

Dinah knelt beside her chair. "I don't know. I've searched everywhere. He simply disappeared without a word. Everyone except me has decided he's dead, but I just don't feel he is. That's one reason I'm going back. If he should be found, I want to be there."

"I don't feel as if he's dead either, so maybe our faith and prayers will restore him to us. Perhaps someone's kidnapped him and is holding him prisoner." She wiped her eyes, but Dinah still detected worry lines around her eyes and mouth. Becky smoothed Dinah's hair. "I'm happy you're home. I've missed both of you."

The news of Dinah's riches couldn't stay a secret, and the neighbors who'd known her all her life converged on the house, partly to welcome her, but mostly to hear news of the gold region.

The young men pelted Seth and Dinah with questions about the possibility of finding gold.

"All of the creeks in the Klondike are staked with claims now, so there's little chance that you can find a good strike. Men like Alex McDonald have bought up many claims, and you might be able to take a lease on one of those," Seth told them.

"Who's Alex McDonald?" Maurie questioned.

"He's a Scot, called the Klondike King, who's reported to be the richest man in the North, maybe in the entire world. He buys claims from men who've grown discouraged or don't have the money for mining equipment," Dinah said.

"It's reported that he owns about three miles of Bonanza and Eldorado," Seth added. "He bought his first claim for four hundred dollars in the fall of ninety-six, struck it rich, and used that gold to buy other claims."

"Let's start out tomorrow!" Vance shouted. "I can't wait to start digging for gold."

Noting the excitement of all the youths around them, Dinah said, "But don't all of you pull up stakes and head north unless you're ready to take the consequences. Are you willing to live where the temperature stays at fifty below zero for weeks? Where it's so cold in the cabin that food stored two feet from the stove freezes? Do you think you can exist for months on sourdough bread and beans? Would you like living in darkness for two or three months out of the year?"

"It didn't seem to hurt you any," a young man commented, with an admiring glance in her direction.

"But you should have seen her when we arrived in Portland last week," Seth said. "It's a hard life, boys, and Dinah is right. Thousands will go to the Klondike, only hundreds will find any gold, and most of those will squander what they find in gambling dens and dance halls."

"Seth," Maurie interrupted, "I can tell that many of these young people will join the stampede in spite of what you've said, so you'd better give them some more hard facts."

"First of all, you'll need lots of money—no less than a thousand dollars. Food is expensive in Dawson. This past winter flour sold for more than a hundred dollars a sack. Assuming that food can be found, a meal of beans, apples, two slices of bread, and coffee costs five dollars. When we left Dawson, flour, bacon, and beans couldn't be bought at any price, and those with supplies had to guard against thieves."

"Seems to me that anyone who finds gold in the Yukon is going to earn it," Maurie commented.

"That's right. And a man with any chronic diseases, such as rheumatism, or one who can't walk thirty miles a day with a fifty-pound load on his back, or who isn't willing to put up with poor food, uncomfortable beds, and unsanitary living conditions had better stay at home."

"I still think if Dinah can do it, so can I," one youth said.

"I disagree. Dinah had lived in Alaska for a year before the stampede started. She'd learned the ways of the North, and she was within forty miles of the Klondike when gold was discovered. Besides, she has more stamina and determination than a dozen men I could name."

Dinah looked at Seth with wondering eyes. Were her ears deceiving her, or had Seth actually paid her a compliment?

*   *   *

To prolong their visit, Maurie and Becky traveled with Dinah, Seth, and Vance to spend the week in Seattle while they bought supplies for their journey. A winter in the Klondike had taught Dinah the important items needed. She helped Vance make a list of provisions.

"You'll need at least a year's supply of food. Copy down these things: lime and lemon juice, lard, black tea, chocolate, salt, candles, rubber boots, mincemeat, dried potatoes, sauerkraut, beans, cornmeal, toilet soap, baking powder, coal oil, lamp chimneys, rope, saws, files, overshoes. And any kind of canned foods you'd like. Remember, though, we'll have to pack these items over the pass, and fifty to seventy pounds is the limit we can carry at one time. We'll need to make several trips, so take only necessities."

As Becky followed them in and out of various stores, noticing the products they bought, she reminisced to Maurie, "It reminds me of what we took with us when we started from Independence with the wagon train for six months."

"Yes, wife, and though I hate to see her go, I'm glad she has her own chance of adventure. We had ours long ago. Now it's Dinah's turn."

"I wonder how much Seth figures in her future? I've tried to find an opening to ask, but she turns my questions aside."

"I can't figure out their relationship, either. It appears to me that they usually don't see eye-to-eye, but that they're on their good behavior now," Maurie admitted. "I like him very much, but he's pretty vague about his past."

Before they went to the hotel dining room for dinner their last evening together, Becky drew Dinah into her room. "Forgive me for acting like a grandmother, dear, but how is it between you and Seth?"

Dinah flushed. "Since Dad disappeared, he's become my self-appointed guardian. He doesn't approve of my tomboyish ways and obviously resents the fact that I made a rich strike on the Eldorado before he did. He thinks women ought to be as they were in the Dark Ages. So if you're worried that he has any romantic designs on me, you can forget that. I'm as safe with him as I am with Grandpa."

"But you're in love with him?"

"Yes, to my sorrow. He treats me as if I'm ten years old."

Looking at Dinah approvingly, Becky said, "Well, if he doesn't think you're a woman when he sees you in that gown, I'll believe the man is blind."

Dinah's hands caressed the pink satin gown she'd bought in Portland. "That's what I had in mind when I ordered it," she admitted with a laugh.

She might as well have worn her old clothes, she thought wryly before the evening ended. Seth spent his time conversing with Maurie and gave Dinah no attention at all. With a laugh, Dinah lifted expressive eyebrows to her grandmother when their glances met. Becky laughed, too, but Dinah detected a sympathetic gleam in her eyes, causing Dinah to wonder if there had been a time when Maurie had ignored her.

Regardless of Seth's inattention, Dinah eagerly looked forward to the journey ahead. As much as she despaired of leaving her grandparents with their sorrow about Nelson's disappearance, Dinah was ready to head north.

Chapter Seven

June 1897

"*L*et's make plans now," Seth suggested the second day after their boat left Seattle. "What are we going to do when we reach Dyea?"

"Fill me in, will you?" Vance said. "We've been moving so fast this last week that I hardly know what's before me."

"Our destination is the Dyea Indian village about nine hundred water miles from Seattle. This ship takes us to Juneau, the capital of Alaska Territory, where we'll board a smaller ship for Dyea at the head of Lynn Canal."

Seth took a crude map from his pocket and handed it to Vance. "From Dyea we cross Chilkoot Pass to Lake Linderman, a distance of thirty miles, but it's the worst part of our journey. Once through the pass, we hope to cross sixty miles of ice to Lake Tagish, then build a boat and go down the Yukon to Dawson. If the ice has melted, it will be necessary to go by boat all the way from Lake Linderman, but the rapids between those lakes are treacherous. We want to avoid them if we can, and we don't have any time to lose."

"How long do you think it will take us?" Vance asked.

"No more than six weeks, if everything goes well," Seth answered.

"And it should, since we're ahead of the big rush."

"Is this the way you and Uncle Nelson went to Alaska?"

"No, we traveled by boat to St. Michael and up the Yukon to Circle City. Not many whites used Chilkoot Pass then."

"It's an old Indian trail used by the Chilkat and Chilkoot Indians for transporting products to trade with the Tagish Indians of the interior," Seth explained.

"Then it must not be too hard to cross," Vance said hopefully.

Seth shook his head. "I hear it's terrible, and we may be foolish to even attempt it," he said with a glance at Dinah, "but it's the shortest, and probably the best route to the Klondike, so Dinah and I agreed to go back that way. There shouldn't be too many people in Dawson City yet, but the stampede will be in full force in a few months."

"And we don't want to leave our claims any longer than we have to," Dinah added.

Healy's Trading Post was the only major building of any size at Dyea, but a few tents and log cabins dotted the landscape. Across the river, opposite the trading post, Dinah saw an Indian encampment.

The rugged mountains they must cross to reach Dawson loomed behind the village. The Dyea River rose in those mountains and flowed through a forest of evergreens and heavy grasses, dividing the beach in half as it entered the shallow inlet.

A small scow transported them from the ship to the beach, where they discovered that their packs had been dumped randomly on the muddy bank. The three of them hurriedly sorted their supplies from the packs of the other passengers. Fortunately, they'd enclosed everything in oilskin bags, or their provisions would have been ruined from the incessant rain they'd endured since leaving Seattle.

They set up two tents on the beach to protect their packs and provide shelter for themselves. Rain mixed with snow fell around them, and Dinah was cold and miserable. For the first time, she wondered if she had the stamina to make this trip to Dawson. But she wouldn't give Seth the satisfaction of knowing her fears, so she gritted her teeth and helped prepare their supper. The smoldering fire sputtered in the rain, providing only enough heat to warm their coffee and the fat pork they tried to fry.

Noting Vance's drawn white face, Dinah realized that he fared worse than she. Last winter in the Klondike had toughened her, but Vance had never faced hardship before. Perhaps more sensitive to their condition than Dinah suspected, Seth motioned to the ship anchored in the inlet.

"That vessel leaves tomorrow for Seattle. It's still not too late to go back. And I'm speaking to both of you," he added, with a piercing look in Dinah's direction.

Vance glanced obliquely at Dinah, and the very fact that she delayed answering Seth indicated forcibly to herself how much she dreaded this trip. She thought of the comforts she could enjoy with her grandparents. She had enough money to last the rest of her life, and living conditions in the Klondike would be miserable. Why then did she hesitate? She had to go back to find out about her father, but being honest with herself, she acknowledged that Seth was the magnet pulling her onward. She wanted to be near him, and she wouldn't consider returning to the States.

She bit her lip, stating decisively, "No. I'm going on."

Vance hesitated momentarily. "If you can make it, Dinah, I surely can. I'd hate to be this close to finding my fortune and turn back because I was afraid to climb that mountain."

"So be it," Seth stated. "If that's the case, we'd better hire some Indians to do our packing for us. Otherwise, we'd have to make several trips up and down the trail, and that could delay us for weeks. I don't doubt that one trip to the pass will be enough for all of us. We'll divide our supplies into seventy-pound packs early in the morning, and when we determine how many packers we'll need, I'll bargain with them. Do you have enough money, Vance? This will be costly."

"Yes. Gramps saw to that. He's been through this himself. I have plenty of gold coins in my money belt."

"Good. The Indians won't take paper money, so you'll need the gold. They charge fifty cents a pound."

Two days later, they left Dyea, tramping behind ten Chilkoot Indians who walked single file in front of them. Along a rambling wagon road they followed a stony creek that crisscrossed acres of willow, spruce, birch, and cottonwood forests.

Vance flashed a smile at Dinah. "This isn't so bad. What beautiful country!"

Dinah nodded, but she couldn't return his smile. She still smarted from the hostile scene with Seth when she'd appeared this morning in her bloomers. He'd stared at her in amazement for a full minute before he finally exploded. "Where'd you find that outfit?"

With a smile that belied the pounding of her heart, she said, "I had it made in Portland. I have another one, too, in case this wears out."

"If you think I'm going to travel with you looking that way, you can think again. Either take those off and put on a skirt, or go on by yourself."

Vance seemed awestruck at the exchange, but he came to Dinah's defense. "I don't think she looks so bad, Seth, and it will be safer for her to wear bloomers while she climbs that mountain. Women wear them in San Francisco."

"It makes no difference what you think. It's a matter of propriety. Mama always taught Janice Sue to adhere to the social mores, even though they might not always be the most convenient."

"Such old-fashioned ideas are exactly why the South lost the Civil War, too," Dinah retorted.

Seth turned angrily toward her, and Dinah backed out of his way.

"And I might remind you, Seth Morgan, that I didn't ask you to accompany me on this trip. I'll make it on my own." Turning to Vance, she said, "You can travel with me or go with Seth. It's up to you."

She faced the packers who had watched the angry exchange in indulgent silence. "I'll start now with the ones who are carrying my supplies."

"Don't you think the two of you are being foolish?" Vance asked. "I don't doubt that any of us can make it to the Klondike on our own, but it will be a lot easier going together."

"And it will be a lot easier for me if I wear these bloomers, and I intend to."

"Have it your way, as usual," Seth said, "but don't blame me if you're jailed when we arrive in Dawson. Remember, that's what Constantine did to some dance-hall girls last winter. And wearing those things puts you in the same class. Janice Sue . . . ."

"Don't mention your sister's name to me again!" Dinah shouted. "If she had the spunk of a rabbit, she'd be out making her own way, like I am, rather than depending on you to send her money. Besides, you haven't seen her for years. You don't know what she's like now."

Seth had made few comments after that exchange, but Dinah often sensed his angry glances as he followed her up the trail. Now that her temper had cooled, Dinah's conscience tortured her. She knew Christians shouldn't lose their tempers in such a manner, but he made her so mad. She could almost hear Susie's admonition, " 'He that is slow to anger is better than the mighty; and he that ruleth his spirit than he that taketh a city.' "

"God," she whispered, "I'm sorry, and I'll try to do better. But I love him so much. Why can't he love me just a little?"

Seth's anger lessened perceptibly as he walked behind Dinah, and he had to admit that her slender figure did look fetching in the bloomers. Rather than detracting from her femininity, the voluminous trousers accentuated her shapely legs, her slight waist, and her erect bearing. In spite of her diminutive size, Dinah carried herself as if she had the world at her command.

"And she almost does," Seth admitted wryly. "I don't know why she can make me so angry, and then I turn around and do just what she wants." But he needed to protect her, and the way she was developing into a woman, men would be flocking around her before long. She'd looked stunning in that pink dinner dress she'd worn in Seattle. He knew that she'd expected him to mention the new dress, but he had to be indifferent toward her. If he wasn't careful, he'd be jumping to her wishes just as Nelson Davis had always done. In plain words, Dinah was a spoiled brat.

After five miles of easy walking, they reached a small settlement where a corduroy bridge brought them to Dyea Canyon, a narrow, two-mile-long chasm. They crossed the river three times, struggling over and around huge rocks, underbrush, and fallen logs. Clearing the canyon, Dinah felt the pull on her ankles and the back of her legs as the trail rose slowly until they reached Sheep Camp, located at the base of the mountains.

The packers moved on undismayed, but the others stopped to catch their breaths, and Dinah looked almost straight upward to the summit, where a small notch marked Chilkoot Pass. A trail of rock and ice overhung with glaciers met her eyes, and a sob escaped her lips. She saw a few miniature figures outlined against the white trail, and when a swirl of fog and snow obliterated the summit, she turned away, tears misting her eyes.

Seth placed his hand on her shoulder and said kindly, "It's only a four-mile climb. You'll make it, but we won't start until tomorrow. We can rest here tonight."

"But they've gone on with our supplies."

"That won't matter. We have our names on them, and the packers will cache them at the top. Nobody will bother them."

Located in a deep basin encircled by the mountains, Sheep Camp's few unpretentious huts teemed with humanity.

"This is the most people we've seen on the trail," Vance said.

"It's where many stampeders stash their supplies and then make several trips up and down the trail to get them. I was told in Dyea that there are facilities here to buy food and for sleeping inside."

One look at the ramshackle buildings dissuaded Dinah, and she said, "I prefer to sleep in my tent, or did the packers take it to the pass?"

"No, it's in my pack," Seth answered. "All three of us can sleep in it tonight."

While Seth and Dinah erected the tent near the trail at some distance from the buildings, Vance went to reconnoiter the place. His face held an amused expression when he returned in a half hour.

"There's quite an assortment of people in the camp. One guy has a printing press that he's taking through the pass, another has forty dozen eggs packed in sand, and one stampeder has several crates of chickens."

"If they manage to take those into Dawson, they'll get more gold than if they try to stake a claim," Dinah said.

"Remember how hungry we were for eggs, Seth, when we arrived in Portland?"

"I also saw three acrobats, as well as a couple of dance-hall girls. One of them calls herself the Dixie Belle, and the other one is Mary Lou." Vance laughed again.

After they ate their meal, Seth said, "I'll go and look over the camp. Do you want to go, Dinah?"

She shook her head. "I'll have all the walking I want to-morrow."

Seth was gone over two hours, and when he returned, his condition alarmed Dinah. His face was gray, and he walked slowly, his head down. He shook like someone with the palsy. When he slumped to the ground, Dinah ran to him.

"What's the matter, Seth? Are you sick?"

He shoved away her hand when she tried to feel his forehead. "No," he said. "Well, yes, I am. It must have been that meat we had for supper. Let's turn in."

He didn't seem to be sick, so what had happened in Sheep Camp to upset him? Had he found the man who'd killed his father? Dinah couldn't think of any other explanation for his strange behavior.

When she was rolled into her blankets and wedged in the tent with the two men, Dinah's mind churned as she contemplated the journey ahead. Could she make it? Was she foolish to think she could accomplish everything she set her head to? Searching for something to bolster her courage, Dinah remembered that the Apostle Paul had once written, "I can do all things through Christ which strengtheneth me." With those words to support her, she finally willed her mind to sleep, for she knew tomorrow would require all the strength she had.

A bitter north wind whistled down from the pass, making it difficult for them to keep a fire going long enough to prepare breakfast. Vance held a blanket to protect the fire while

Dinah fried eggs and bacon and brewed coffee. Seth, who seemed as usual this morning, rolled up the tent and secured their backpacks. Dinah wondered what had ailed him the night before, but whatever it was, it must not have been his stomach, for his appetite was as keen as ever.

Although she berated herself as a coward, Dinah hadn't looked up to the pass that morning. After she finished eating, she sighed inwardly and surveyed the trail. To her dismay, Chilkoot Pass didn't look any less formidable this morning. A haze of fog and blowing snow covered the pass. Momentarily, the haze dissipated and she saw where the trail disappeared through the high, narrow gap. To the left of the pass, a shiny blue glacier dominated a jagged peak. Already the trail was dotted with stampeders.

I'll climb it or die in the attempt, Dinah thought as she strapped on her backpack. When she straightened from an inspection of her shoelaces to be sure they were secure, she saw two women walking toward them.

Two beautiful women, she deduced when the women came abreast of them.

"Good morning," the tallest of the two said in a silky voice. "Are you gentlemen going our way?"

She flashed Seth a bold glance and favored Vance with a smile. She ignored Dinah.

Seth seemed angry at the encounter and didn't answer, but Vance laughed. "You aren't thinking about crossing the pass?"

"Indeed, we are. We've been told this is the quickest way to Dawson City, and that town sounds like the place for the Dixie Belle to make her fortune."

Dinah wondered if the two women actually expected to try the trail garbed as they were in silk gowns and velvet capes. Leather slippers peeked out from beneath their long skirts. They carried heavy packs, and Dinah figured they expected Seth and Vance to help them.

Seth motioned to Dinah to follow him, and they set out with Vance bringing up the rear.

"Good luck, girls," Vance called. "It's everybody for himself on this trail."

When she knew the two women couldn't hear her, Dinah said over her shoulder, "I thought you'd been taught to be chivalrous to ladies."

"I'm not sure they're ladies. Besides, if I get Vance Miller through Chilkoot Pass, that's all I'll be able to do."

"Do you know who they are, Vance?"

"Those dance-hall girls I mentioned last night—Dixie Belle and Mary Lou."

Dinah heard the two women chatting and laughing behind them for a while until she outdistanced them. Facing the greatest challenge of her life, she soon forgot the women. The six miles they'd climbed to Sheep Camp had been no problem at all, compared to this icy trail packed solidly by those who'd gone before them. Blood pounded in her ears, and she often gasped for breath. Screaming gusts of snow surrounded them, and the bitter cold numbed her face, but inside her woolen garments, her body sizzled with heat.

She refused to look at the heights around her or to contemplate the danger if she should slip and fall. She kept her eyes on Seth's broad shoulders bent beneath the weight of the pack. As the trail ascended, Seth slowed his pace.

A few wide spots in the trail offered resting places, and Dinah longed to stop, but she refused to voice her need to Seth. When he did finally step aside into one of the rest areas, she flopped on the ground and panted. Vance was quite a distance behind them, and Dinah stifled a scream when he slipped to his knees and floundered on the sheer face of the mountain. Although Seth looked tired, he dropped his pack and hurried, as fast as the icy trail allowed, to help Vance.

Taking Vance's pack, he pulled the younger man to his

feet and assisted him up the trail to where Dinah lay. Vance sprawled on his back and closed his eyes, too weary to speak. Dinah didn't waste any energy on words, either, for they still had a long distance to go before they'd reach the summit. She felt she'd hardly rested at all when Seth touched her on the shoulder.

"We'll have to move on. Can you make it, Vance?"

Vance struggled to a sitting position. "Sure. I'm rested now, but I thought I was a goner an hour ago. I'm going to climb this mountain. I couldn't look Gramps in the face if I turned back now."

Dinah smiled slightly. She knew how he felt. She'd grown up listening to her grandparents' tales of the difficulties they'd faced crossing the overland trail to Oregon. She'd have a few stories of her own to tell now. But first she had to reach that pass.

Behind them on the trail, she saw that the Dixie Belle and her companion were now accompanied by several men.

"I see our lady travelers found some helpers who were more susceptible to their charms than you and Vance," Dinah said.

Seth glanced down the trail, and a disgusted look crossed his face. "Dinah, you'd be better off to ignore those women. Let's keep ahead of them."

Feeling the sharp wind blowing from the mountain peaks and squinting to filter the occasional flash of dazzling sunlight upon the snow, Dinah soon forgot everything except her need to climb the mountain. The rest had helped, though, and she plodded upward, frequently glancing over her shoulder to be sure Vance was keeping up.

Her cousin's features looked drawn, and every step seemed to be an effort, but his face displayed the determination she'd often seen his grandfather show when confronted with some difficulty. Strange to think that the stubbornness that had prompted Matt Miller to give up everything he owned to cross the continent in 1844 and later enabled him to build a prosperous steamboat empire on the Sacramento River in California lived in Vance Miller as he scaled the Chilkoot Pass in 1897. Was it true that history repeated itself? Or did every generation have the opportunity to prove its mettle?

The backpack felt as if it weighed a ton, and her skin burned where the straps crossed her shoulders. The muscles of her legs and back stretched taut as a spring. Dinah had lost all sense of time before they reached the Scales, a place where Indian packers weighed freight.

Seth motioned them to rest again, and tears stung Dinah's eyes as she looked at the last ascent.

Vance glanced upward and gulped before he stretched out on the ground and covered his face. The trail appeared perpendicular, and those who climbed it looked as if they were suspended in space. A stampeder lost his footing and slid back down the trail, landing almost at their feet.

"I can't make it," Vance said.

"Sure you can," Dinah encouraged. "That man fell, but look at those who have reached the summit and are going through the pass."

"It's only another thousand feet or so, but I don't think we dare try it today," Seth said. "Let's set up our tent and start out early in the morning. I'm tired, too, Vance. It's nothing to be ashamed of."

They'd been in camp more than an hour when the dancehall girls and their companions arrived. Some of the men had long since taken the women's packs, while two others pushed and pulled to help them negotiate the trail. Both women wailed when they passed the campfire where Dinah rested.

Despite their profession, Dinah felt sorry for the women. Based on her own suffering, she realized the agony they must be enduring. She'd been bred on hardship, but these women apparently hadn't. Noting that Seth talked to the

Indian packers who'd taken their supplies to the summit, Dinah took the extra coffee left from their supper and went to where the two women lay in the snow.

Lifting Dixie Belle's head, she said, "Here, drink some of this coffee, and you'll feel better."

The woman groaned, but lifted her head enough to drink. "Thanks," she muttered. "That did help. Give some to Mary Lou. She's in worse shape than I am."

After giving the other woman some coffee, Dinah buttered bread they'd brought from Dyea and took it to them.

They leaned on their elbows to eat, and Dixie said to Dinah, "How come you're able to take this climb? You're not as big as I am."

"I've lived in Alaska for over two years. I'm accustomed to cold and snow, but this trail is the worst thing I've tackled."

"You've got a heart of gold, dearie," Mary Lou mumbled. "Thanks."

The men who'd accompanied the women had put up a tent for them, and they crawled into it.

Seth stood by their tent when Dinah returned, and he said, "I doubt that you have a heart of gold, but you've got a hard head. I told you to keep away from them."

She didn't answer him, but scooted into the tent and went to sleep. She didn't even hear Vance and Seth when they came to bed, but they were gone the next morning when she awakened. She slid out of her bedroll, groaning at the pain in her body, and inched toward the tent flap.

She wiped her eyes to be sure she wasn't still asleep. In front of the tent where the two dance-hall women had slept, Seth stood deep in conversation with Dixie Belle. They were too far away to hear their words, nor could she see Seth's face, but Dixie listened intently to him. Finally, the woman shook her head, laughed slightly, and standing on tiptoe, she kissed Seth on the lips and went back into the tent.

Seth stood as if he'd been turned to stone, and Dinah

dropped the flap before he could turn and see her staring at him. Why would he be talking to Dixie when he'd told her to stay away from the woman? Had he been warning the Dixie Belle to leave Dinah alone? Or was there a side to Seth Morgan that she didn't know about? He'd seemed immune to any feminine charms that she possessed, and she'd never known him to show interest in any of the women in Circle, so what had stimulated his interest in this dance-hall girl? Dinah stifled the sob that threatened the little composure she had left.

Hearing his step near the tent, Dinah lay quietly, unable to face him at this point. Instinct told her that this was one thing she didn't dare mention to Seth. When she heard crackling fire and smelled frying bacon, Dinah emerged from the tent.

The effort to stand was so painful that she fell back on her haunches with the first try.

"Walk around, and your joints will loosen up," Seth said.

Vance hobbled toward her and lifted her upward. "We both had the same trouble, but it isn't so bad once you walk some."

The sun shone brightly, and Dinah hoped for a more pleasant day than yesterday, but her optimism was blighted when she faced the last lap of the trail. They waited while a string of Indian packers walked by, their faces and bodies showing no strain at all.

Seth had procured three canes, and Dinah did find the staff helped as she started up the steps that had been cut into the snow and ice. Before she had climbed far, Dinah's head ached, and her lungs burned from the exertion at such a high elevation. Her heart pounded unmercifully, but she kept plodding upward. She didn't know how many times she slid and fell, and often she crawled on her hands and knees, actually feeling safer in that position.

She had eyes for no one, thoughts for nothing except gaining the pass. If Vance didn't make it, she was powerless to help him, so she kept climbing. A strong wind blew sleet and snow around her, and most of the time she couldn't even see Seth a few feet ahead. Occasionally, a man passed by, sliding downhill on his bottom. These were the stampeders who couldn't afford to hire Indian packers and had to make innumerable trips up and down the trail.

Dinah fell again and didn't have the strength to struggle to her feet, so she crawled forward. A welcome hand took her arm and pulled upward.

"We made it!" Seth said. Mixed with the fatigue in his voice, she heard the joy of accomplishment he felt.

When he released her arm, Dinah fell to her knees again.

"Vance?" she whispered.

"I'll drop off this pack and go look for him. Don't move."

"As if I could," she murmured. Concern for Vance kept her from complete collapse, and she looked around the narrow pass. To the north, sun glittered on the dazzling peaks, and the shadowy mountainsides loomed mysterious and inviting. In spite of the ruggedness, the path toward Lake Linderman looked easy after scaling Chilkoot Pass. Hearing a sound to her left, Dinah turned to see Vance limping into view with Seth by his side. She leaned her head on the pack and stretched out to relax her tired muscles.

Chapter Eight

July 1897

"Will the trail be any easier now?" Vance asked the next morning when they packed to resume their journey.

"We don't have any more mountains like that one, but we have many difficulties ahead," Seth said. "For one thing, I don't know the trail, but I've hired a Chilkat Indian to guide us. We need to cross three lakes connected by rivers. The water is frozen and probably won't thaw for weeks, but we must be extremely cautious to stay out of soft places where we might fall through the ice. Most of the stampeders will stop at one of the first two lakes to build boats and wait for the thaw. If you're game, we'll head for Lake Tagish, the third one."

"I don't know anything about this. I'd be lost in ten minutes if I were on my own. Do what you think best," Vance said.

"This plan still all right with you, Dinah?"

"The sooner we arrive in Dawson the happier I'll be," she said shortly, and Seth looked at her curiously.

"Then let's pack our sleds and prepare to leave. There's

another group of travelers who want to join us, so we won't be completely alone."

When Dinah saw that their fellow travelers included Dixie Belle and Mary Lou, she stared at Seth, but he turned away to avoid her eyes.

Later, when she and Vance were alone, she said, "Why does he tell me to stay away from those women when he allows them to travel with us?"

"You'll have to ask Seth. I'm surprised myself that he wants to take them."

"Maybe he didn't know the women were going along."

"Yes, he did. As a matter of fact, he approached the men who've befriended the women and asked them if they'd like to join our party. That big man, Joe Arthur, is going to start a dance hall in Dawson, and the two women will work for him."

"It doesn't matter to me, but I can't imagine why Seth is being deceitful about it."

"You'll have to ask him if you want to know."

She didn't ask him, although she seethed inwardly at Seth. He didn't pay any attention to Dixie, but Dinah couldn't forget that the woman had kissed him. However, the five days of travel from Lake Linderman to Tagish proved so grueling that she didn't have the energy to worry about Seth's actions. Before the first day passed, the dance-hall women played out, and the men took turns pulling them on sleds.

By the end of the second day, the harness that Dinah wore over her shoulders to pull the sled had galled her flesh. She padded the irritated spots, but the harness continued to burden her. At times, Dinah's muscles throbbed so painfully from tugging the sled that she wanted to scream. On the third morning, Seth removed part of her load and added it to his sled.

"You put that back," she said crossly. "Your load is already heavier than mine."

"You're almost worn out now, and we still have three days before we reach Lake Tagish. You're not built for this type of travel."

She knew he was right, but she went to his sled and retrieved her packs. Mustering every ounce of willpower she possessed, Dinah walked rapidly all day. The sight of the other women riding on sleds worked on her spirit like a catalyst, and she plunged onward.

When they finally camped, Dinah put up her tent immediately and crawled into it. She didn't care if she ever moved again. She was asleep when Vance brought her supper. He shook her slightly to awaken her and made the mistake of touching her sore back.

"Oh!" she screamed, "Don't touch me."

"I'm sorry, Dinah. Seth told me to bring you some food." He helped her sit up. "My shoulders and back are sore, too. As children, when we dreamed about finding gold, we didn't realize how much that gold would cost, did we?"

Groggy from sleep, Dinah merely shook her head. Eating took more effort than it was worth, but she knew she had to have food.

"Wonder why we're doing this, Dinah. Gramps will leave me all the money I'll ever need, and you've already made a fortune. Why are we putting ourselves in so much misery?"

"Love of adventure seems to be born and bred in us, Vance. Our grandparents were pioneers, and we want to be, too. I couldn't be content to sponge off my relatives the rest of my life. Could you?"

"No, I guess not. If I strike it rich, I intend to pay Gramps for the grubstake he gave me. I want to be my own man."

"Same way with me. I'm not willing to become the chattel of any man I might marry. I want to be independent."

Seth stuck his head into the tent, and Dinah wondered if he'd heard her remark.

"Finished eating?"

She nodded her head, and he crawled into the tent.

"I'll go wash the pans," Vance said.

After Vance left, Seth said, "Take off your shirt and turn over on your stomach."

Dinah flashed a startled look in his direction.

"I won't . . . ," she started, but Seth demanded, "I said take off your shirt, and I don't want any argument. I want to look at your back and shoulders."

Dinah turned her back to him and pulled the shirt over her head, stifling a moan as she lifted her arms. Holding the shirt over her breasts, she loosened the straps of her chemise to let it fall around her waist.

Seth whistled. "Why didn't you tell me what had happened to your back? I'm going to rub ointment on these raw spots. It will hurt you, but I'll be as gentle as I can."

"Do your shoulders hurt?"

"Of course they hurt. I don't have any galled places, but my back is tired. I don't know why you can't admit that you aren't invincible. It isn't weakness to acknowledge that there are some things you can't do."

"I don't need a sermon, Seth."

His hands on her shoulders were gentle, and the salve brought a soothing relief to her aching muscles. In spite of herself, tears slipped from Dinah's eyes, and she began to sob. Seth ignored her tears until he finished his ministrations. He covered her with a blanket.

"I'll rub your back again in the morning and put some compresses on the broken places, but it might be best for you to sleep without clothing tonight. I'll be close by; nobody will come in on you. Also, I'm taking part of your load the rest of this trip, and I don't want any argument about it. Understand?"

She refused to answer him, and with a slight laugh, he gathered her into his arms, blanket and all, and held her until she stopped sobbing. Dinah wished he would never let her go, and she had a brief insight into what it could mean to turn to a man for comfort and strength. Maybe dependence wouldn't be so bad if the man were Seth Morgan.

Seth smoothed back her hair and looked into her moist blue eyes. "Feel better now, Crybaby?" he said teasingly.

Dinah twisted out of his arms, and with a laugh, Seth hurried out of the tent before she could voice the stinging retort on her lips.

After Seth applied ointment the next morning and laid heavy bandages on the abrasions, the harness didn't bother Dinah much. When they stopped for their midday rest, Seth asked, "Any better this morning?"

"Yes, thank you," Dinah said shortly, and she took her pan of food and wandered away from the rest of them. Dinah leaned against a spruce tree while she ate, inhaling with pleasure the fragrant odor of the evergreen. She knew she wasn't showing the proper gratitude, but the man could make her so angry. Last night she'd thought he held her with affection, only to have him call her a crybaby.

Brooding over Seth's attitude, Dinah didn't realize she wasn't alone until Joe Arthur hunkered down beside her.

"Lonesome?"

"No, I'm not."

The man hadn't spoken to her before, but he'd given Dinah the eye more than once, and she didn't like being alone with him. Realizing that she was out of sight of the others, she started to her feet, but Arthur laid his hand on her arm.

"No need to hurry off. I want to talk to you."

Dinah saw Seth rushing toward them. "Arthur, I told you Dinah was off-limits to you and your party. If you don't want to stick to that agreement, you can travel alone."

He reached a hand to help Dinah to her feet. "Come, Dinah. It's time to hit the trail."

A stinging rebuke came to Dinah's lips, but because she didn't want Joe Arthur's attentions, she stifled it. She'd be safer to acknowledge Seth as her guardian.

The temperature warmed perceptibly by the time they reached Lake Tagish, and the ice and snow turned mushy. In a few places, the Indian guide had warned about spots where they might have broken through the ice, but with his help, they negotiated the trail safely. High cliffs surrounded Lake Tagish on three sides, but low foothills at the northern end of the lake framed the outlet into Tagish River.

Upon their arrival at the lake, Seth said, "We can slow down for a few days. The ice breakup probably won't come for another week, so we'll have time to build our boats."

"How much longer to Dawson?" Arthur asked.

"Less than two weeks, once we start."

"So we should arrive there around the first of July."

"That's my calculation."

With only fifteen people in the party, the group decided that three boats would accommodate all of them and their baggage. The boats amounted to little more than barges with sails, and Dinah wondered if they'd wreck when they went through Miles Canyon and the Whitehorse Rapids that she'd heard about. She doubted if Seth knew any more about building boats than she did.

In spite of Seth's protests, Dinah worked on the boats along with the men. Her hands and eyes burned while she punched tar and hemp into the cracks of the boat, but she never considered stopping. Dixie and Mary Lou lounged in front of their tent and watched the workers, but they didn't offer to help.

More than once Dinah considered asking Seth if that was

the kind of "lady" he wanted her to be, but for some reason she held her tongue.

When she wasn't working, Dinah kept to herself, not talking with anyone except Vance. The ice started to melt before they finished the boats, for which Dinah was thankful. She wanted to arrive at Dawson as soon as possible. Three months of Seth's constant company had shattered her composure. Another encounter like that one in her tent would loosen her tongue, and she'd blurt out how she felt about him. He'd laugh at that, too, she supposed.

The evening before they left Lake Tagish, Dinah walked downstream to watch the large blocks of ice bobbing up and down in the current. She questioned the wisdom of starting out with the river so full of ice, but Seth seemed determined to move on immediately.

As she stared pensively at the water, she wondered if Seth was attracted to Dixie. He had ignored her all the time they'd been at Lake Tagish, almost too obvious in his avoidance, as if he didn't trust himself to even speak to the woman. As far as that was concerned, he'd avoided Dinah, too, although he eyed her like a hawk if any of the other men spoke to her.

Startled from her thoughts by a sound behind her, Dinah whirled quickly to face Dixie Belle. To be fair, Dinah couldn't blame any man for being attracted to the woman. In spite of her profession—perhaps because of it—Dixie was a beauty. Even with the hardships of this journey she had remained neat and clean, and each day she came from her tent in beautiful garments. Dinah couldn't help compare Dixie's appearance to how she must look in her bloomers.

"I'm sorry I startled you," Dixie said in her slow, soft voice.

"No matter. I'm having second thoughts about the wisdom of being on the river in our flimsy boats. There are dangerous rapids between here and Dawson."

"Have you traveled this way before?"

"No, but I've talked to miners who've been through this country, and they've told me some hair-raising tales about their experiences. Seth thinks it safe enough, but we don't always agree."

"Have you known Seth long?" Dixie asked unconcernedly, with too much indifference to be natural, Dinah thought.

"We met him when we moved to Alaska in eighteen ninety-five. He was a friend of my father."

"Was?"

"My father disappeared several months ago. We don't know what happened to him."

"So Seth's taking care of you now?"

"He may think he is, but I'm able to take care of myself."

Suddenly Seth was beside them, and he said sharply to Dinah, while he ignored Dixie completely, "What do you mean wandering off alone like this?"

"Oh, but I'm not alone."

"Vance said you left by yourself. Come on back."

"What could possibly bother me? There's no one else in miles of us."

"How do you know you can trust these men who're traveling with us? I don't like the way Arthur watches you."

All of the indignation Dinah had harbored against Seth since she'd suspected his interest in Dixie surfaced, and she faced him angrily.

"Don't you ever question anything I do again, Seth Morgan! I happen to know that you invited this group to travel with us, and if you didn't think they were fit companions for me, why ask them? And I'll stay out here all night if I want to. Leave me alone."

Seth stared at her a moment, too angry to answer, then turned on his heel and left.

"You're in love with him, aren't you?" Dixie said with a laugh once Seth was out of hearing.

Dinah didn't answer, but turned away to stare at the river.

After a few minutes she heard Dixie head back toward the camp.

Six weeks after they'd left Portland, they arrived at Dawson, and Dinah had a sense of homecoming as they swung around a rocky bluff and Dawson spread before her. The Klondike River roared into the Yukon, and she looked with fondness at the tapering mountain beyond the river, with the great slide slashed across its surface forming a backdrop for the town at its feet.

"Look how the town has expanded," Dinah said to Seth in the first words they'd exchanged since their stormy encounter at Lake Tagish.

"And still growing, from the sound of Ladue's sawmill."

Tents, shacks, and log cabins sprawled haphazardly along the right bank of the Yukon for about a mile in the direction of the low, stunted trees marking the high hills rising back of the town. A few unfinished buildings stood near the river, and Dinah said, "One of those should be my hotel. I'd hoped it was nearer completion than that."

"Which town is Dawson?" Vance asked, indicating a village on the low, swampy sandbar south of the Klondike River.

"That one is Louse Town," Seth said. "It was an Indian village before the gold strike."

"I see the Mounties are well established." Dinah pointed to the Canadian flag flying over a low barracks near the river.

Hundreds of men converged on the riverbank to meet them when they tied their boats among a few others already docked. The men hailed Dixie Belle and Mary Lou with obvious delight, while Dinah, under Seth's stern glance, attracted scant attention.

"Got anything to sell?" one man called.

"We need everything here. Food, medicine, liquor," another miner said.

Joe Arthur smiled. "We can accommodate you if you'll give us a few days to settle in. Make way for the ladies," he said as he guided the two women up the bank.

After they made arrangements to cache the majority of their supplies for a few days, Dinah said, "Vance, I'm going to check with Ladue to see when he will have my hotel finished, and then we'll leave for the claim."

At Ladue's she learned that her hotel would be ready for occupancy in two weeks. As she left his office, Joe Arthur intercepted her.

"Now that I've caught you without your guardian angel, I have a business proposition to make. You have a hotel nearly finished; I need a place to open my saloon. Can we make a deal?"

So Arthur had no amorous designs on her. He simply coveted her real estate.

"I doubt it. What do you have in mind?"

"You run the hotel, I'll operate a saloon and dance hall downstairs. Ladue says you're building a commodious structure."

Dinah had a sudden notion to become partners with Arthur just to spite Seth, but she said, "Sorry, Mr. Arthur, that isn't the type of establishment I intend to operate. You'll have to find another building."

She didn't know what Seth planned to do, nor did she ask him, but when she came from her meetings with Ladue and Arthur, he waited with Vance, packs ready to travel.

"There's going to be a lot of disappointed people this summer," Seth commented. "I talked to Ogilvie, and he said every inch of the Bonanza, Eldorado, and several other nearby streams is staked. Unless there are strikes made on other creeks, all of the stampeders behind us won't find any riches. Ogilvie has already surveyed more than a hundred claims on the Bonanza, and almost that many on the Eldorado."

"Did he find any problem with the size of our claims?"

"No," Seth admitted. "You did a good job of measuring."

"I'm sure glad you made a claim for me, Dinah, or I wouldn't have anything, either," Vance said.

"Let's hope that Susie and Waldo have been able to save it for you."

Vance became more and more excited during their eighteen-mile journey, for they saw gold glistening in gravel dumps, in sluice boxes, in open shafts.

When the travelers came in sight of Dinah's claim, they saw Susie and Waldo sitting on chairs in front of the cabin. The older people rushed to greet them.

After one disbelieving look at Dinah's bloomers, Susie hugged her tightly. "Honey, am I glad to see you!"

"Is anything wrong?" Dinah asked quickly.

"No, no. We've dug more gold than we know what to do with, and we've kept Mr. Vance's claim intact." She released Dinah and turned to Vance.

"So you're Matt's grandson. You favor him, but I hope you don't act like him. He was a contrary man."

"I can be contrary, too, but Gramps isn't like that anymore."

"I'd heard he'd changed, but I'll have to see it to believe it."

"Tell us all the news," Seth said as Susie rustled around to set food before them. Bathsheba jumped on Dinah's lap and purred contentedly as Dinah stroked her.

"We're more interested in what's going on Outside, but we'll tell ours first," Waldo said.

"There's more gold in this country than San Francisco ever thought of having," Susie started. "And prices have gone sky-high. We've started keeping the dogs inside with us at night, afraid they'll be stolen. Dogs sell for more than a thousand dollars. In Dawson, a piece of pie costs seventy cents, a bowl of mush and coffee is a dollar, and you have to pay more than three dollars for a steak."

"That is, if you can get them. Food is scarce in Dawson," Waldo added.

"How has your food held out?" Seth asked.

"Not bad, but we could use some fresh things."

"We brought in supplies and have many more coming through St. Michael. They won't get here for several weeks, though," Seth said.

"Stampeders started arriving in April, sledding in from Dyea," Waldo continued. "They brought a few supplies, and prices skyrocketed. One man had a ready-cooked turkey, and it raffled for one hundred seventy-four dollars."

"Any more gold strikes?" Seth asked.

"Claims are being staked on Bear, Hunker, Gold Bottom, and other tributaries of the Klondike. A new town, Grand Forks, has built up at the junction of the Eldorado and the Bonanza."

"Yes, we passed by that," Dinah said.

"And you know those lots that you bought from Ladue for five hundred dollars each? He's asking five thousand now for lots—and getting it. Do you want to sell yours?" Waldo asked.

"No, although a man stopped me on the street and tried to buy the property, unfinished building and all. Another man offered to go in with me as a partner."

"Who was that?" Seth demanded.

"Joe Arthur."

"I told him to stay away from you. What did you tell him?"

Dinah couldn't resist retorting, "Seth, if you didn't want that man around me, why did you invite him to travel with us?"

"I had my reasons, but it had nothing to do with you."

But I surely would like to know why you asked him, Dinah thought. Did Seth suspect Arthur had something to do with his father's death, and wanted to watch him?

"I told him I didn't want a partner. I'm sure there will be

plenty of saloons and dance halls in Dawson, but I don't want to be under the same roof with one."

"This all sounds like Gramps's stories of San Francisco," Vance said. "I'll have to write him all about it."

"Knowing him like I do, I wouldn't be surprised if Matt showed up here anyway," Susie said.

"But he's almost ninety years old!" Dinah protested.

"I doubt that would stop Matt," Susie insisted.

"A lot of dance halls and saloons are building up," Waldo observed. "Seems like the sinners always flock in first. But that priest, William Judge, has built his hospital, and a few nuns are helping him. He has a little mission church, too, so the Lord's word is being sounded forth."

"There's a lot of good people in Dawson," Susie said, "and it's too bad they don't have somewhere decent to go besides dance halls and saloons."

"As soon as my hotel is in operation, they'll have a decent place. And in my spare time I'll help Father Judge take care of his patients."

"Now it's your turn. What's new Outside?" Waldo asked.

Reaching in her bag, Dinah handed him a certificate of credit from the Portland bank. "You're rich, for one thing."

Susie shouted when she saw the total of $60,000. "And we've that much more stashed around here that we've found in the three months you've been gone."

"And here's some fresh tea for you."

Susie immediately stirred up the flames in the stove and heated water.

Dinah went to the kennels behind the cabin for a joyous reunion with Shadrach, Meshach, and Abednego. After the men left to show Vance his claim and explain mining procedures, Susie came to where Dinah sat with the dogs, nuzzling her face in their soft fur.

"Thinking about your pa?"

"Yes. I can't believe he's dead, and neither does my grandmother. Have you had any news at all from him? I'd hoped he'd be here when I got back."

"Nothing. I think you might as well give up, Dinah. If he were alive, you'd have heard by now."

"I realize that, but I thought there was a slight chance he might have been hurt and hadn't been able to send me word. I can't give him up, Susie."

Eager to start working on his claim, Vance didn't want to take time to build a cabin.

"There's no reason I can't live in a tent this summer," Seth said. "If you move in with Waldo at your claim, Susie, that would leave room for Vance with Dinah."

"I'll be in Dawson by cold weather anyway," Dinah said, "and you and Vance can live here."

Seth and Dinah helped Vance start his claim the next day, showing him the steps needed to reach the first pay streak. Before the month was out, Jack and Nannie Crow walked into view. Dinah ran to meet them.

"How'd you know we were back?"

"Didn't know, just came by to see," Nannie said.

"How are things with the tribe?"

"Not good," she answered. "Much sickness of the children. White man's sickness."

"Mostly caused by the *nahani*, we think," Jack added.

"*Nahani?*"

"Evil spirits. A new one came to our woods a few months ago. It wanders around crying, never stays in one place. Like a lost soul," Nannie said solemnly.

Dinah remembered that they'd told her before about these mysterious *nahanis* inhabiting the forest, and she dismissed their comments as sheer superstition. If the children were sick, though, she'd share some of the medicine she'd brought from Portland.

"Come and meet my cousin Vance, and plan to stay a few days."

Although the Indians helped Dinah with many things, they'd never shown any interest in her gold mining, obviously thinking the white man's drudgery for gold was much work for nothing. They sat on the bank and watched the three Americans shovel the hard ground.

"We must have worked faster than I thought," Seth said. "It's getting dark already."

At his words, Jack bounded up from his leaning position and pointed westward. A dark streak partially obscured the sun, and as they watched, blackness slowly enveloped it.

"A solar eclipse," Seth said in awe. "Don't look directly at it."

Nannie dropped to her knees, moaning, and Jack covered his eyes. The wail of the malamutes caused the hair to rise on Dinah's neck. Carefully shielding her eyes, she gazed at the impressive sight. The moon's shadow appeared on the western edge of the sun and moved slowly across its surface. At the moment of total eclipse, a brilliant halo flashed into view around the obscure orb.

"Ah, how beautiful!" Seth said.

Dinah turned from her contemplation of the sun to stare at Seth as he continued, " 'The heavens declare the glory of God; and the firmament sheweth his handywork. Day unto day uttereth speech, and night unto night sheweth knowledge. There is no speech nor language, where their voice is not heard. Their line is gone out through all the earth, and their words to the end of the world. In them hath he set a tabernacle for the sun.' "

"Seth, that was beautiful."

Seth shook his head and looked at her. "Yes, beautiful."

He must think she referred to the eclipse. Had the natural phenomenon startled him out of his unbelief in God? Dinah was heartened to know that deep in his soul, Seth's faith in God still burned. Only a spark was needed to kindle it into flame. Surely the majesty of the northland would do that.

Although the sun now shone brightly and the malamutes had stopped wailing, Jack and Nannie still crouched in fear.

"Come, my friends, don't be afraid. It's just a natural thing of nature."

"No. No," Jack said. "Evil things happen. Bad weather ahead. Much sickness. Winter comes early."

No use to argue with them, Dinah knew, and when she went into Dawson a few weeks later, the town's residents seemed struck with the same malady that ailed the Crows. Hordes of men patrolled the streets, demanding to buy food.

Dinah stopped by the Mounties' barracks, and Timothy greeted her with pleasure. He presented her to Captain Constantine. "You remember Miss Davis, Captain? She paid us a brief visit at Fortymile last year."

"It's not a good time for you to be in town, Miss," Constantine admonished her. "General panic is affecting everyone. We've had hundreds of men come to this town without adequate supplies for the winter, and there's no food to be had."

"I noticed a long line at the A. C. Trading Company."

"The clerks admit only one man at a time, and when he gets inside there's precious little to buy," Constantine said. "They'll sell only a few days' supplies to each person. A man can have a million dollars in gold and still be unable to purchase enough food to keep from starving. I've written to Ottawa that we're facing a crisis, but what can the government do?"

"We're all mighty helpless in the face of a Yukon winter," Timothy said.

"And if the Indians' predictions are true, winter will set in early," Constantine added. "Do you have enough supplies, Miss? If not, you'd better take the next boat out of here."

"Last week's boat brought my hotel fixtures and the supplies we'd ordered before we left Seattle. We purchased enough to feed five adults, as well as food for my restaurant, but we won't have an overabundance."

"So you're the young lady who'll be running the Yukon Hotel."

"Yes. I'm moving to town next week."

"What about your claim?" Timothy asked.

"My cousin and Seth Morgan are taking a lay on it. I wasn't keen on digging for any more gold, and they can mine my claim as well as theirs."

"I, for one, will be pleased to welcome you to Dawson," Timothy said with a meaningful smile.

"Will you have any chaperon, Miss?" Constantine asked. "There are some pretty rough characters in town now."

"I'm used to looking after myself, sir. I'll be all right."

"We'll keep an eye on you," Timothy assured her, and Dinah wished that she could return the obvious affection mirrored in his eyes.

Chapter Nine

Fall 1897–Winter 1898

*B*y the last of August, when ice an inch thick formed in gold pans, Dinah realized that the early winter predicted by the Indians had become a reality. Since Dinah's living quarters at the hotel had been completed, she moved into Dawson, leaving the cabin for Seth and Vance.

Ten thousand people had swarmed to the Klondike during the summer, and reports circulated that hordes of other gold seekers would soon arrive. This news pleased Dinah, for a large population would insure a successful hotel business.

"It isn't good news, Dinah," Timothy told her when he came to visit on her first day at the hotel. "Captain Constantine has sent Mounties to Chilkoot Pass, Lake Tagish, and downriver to Circle City and Fort Yukon to stop the cheechakos."

"Cheechakos?"

"Newcomers, greenhorns. It's what these stampeders are being called. It's a derivative of some Indian words meaning 'to approach.' "

"We have a lot of cheechakos already."

"Yes, and the Mounties are warning those without enough

food for the winter to leave immediately. The stores open only one hour a day now. Flour, bacon, and beans, the items most needed by the miners, can't be bought at any price. The captain predicts that within a month the trading companies will have nothing to sell."

"Surely there will be more boats before the final freeze," Dinah suggested.

"Perhaps," Timothy said, without much enthusiasm. "The irony of the whole situation is that the safes of the three trading companies are packed with gold. Even a room at our barracks is piled to the ceiling with nuggets and gold dust left there by miners for safekeeping."

"But you can't eat gold!"

"Exactly," Timothy agreed. "And while the cheechakos haven't paid much attention to the Mounties, they have been frightened by Indian scouts who keep warning, 'White man must leave. No more boats to bring food.' "

"We may be facing a bleak winter."

"I suppose you wouldn't consider leaving?" Timothy asked, concern in his voice.

With a smile, Dinah merely shook her head.

Joe Arthur had built his saloon and dance hall, the Golden Nugget, directly across the street from Dinah's hotel. Had he done this to irritate her because she hadn't accepted his proposition? When Arthur met her on the street with Dixie Belle on his arm, she decided he had done just that.

Arthur doffed his hat and bowed. "Good morning, Miss Davis. Guess we're going to be neighbors even if we couldn't be partners. I hope we won't be too noisy for your guests."

"That remains to be seen." Dixie hadn't spoken, but Dinah turned from Arthur and said amicably to her, "Has Dawson lived up to your expectations?"

"It's pretty crude now, but it has possibilities. I am worried about this winter, though. I don't think I'll like days of total darkness, and if we run out of food, it will be terrible."

"I have plenty of supplies," Arthur said.

"But we can't eat liquor, Joe. I wish you'd stocked in more food and less whiskey."

He flashed an angry glance at her and stifled a retort.

"If you get hungry I'll share my food with you while it lasts, Miss," Dinah said. "You know where I am."

As Dinah moved away, Dixie voiced her gratitude, and although Dinah resented Seth's interest in this woman, she did consider Dixie a cut above most dance-hall girls. Once the woman had obviously lived a decent life, which she wasn't doing now. Arthur treated her as if he owned her, and he probably did.

Dinah's hotel opened in mid-September, and because she had one of the few stocks of good food in town, long queues formed in front of the hotel long before her kitchen crew had the meals ready. Dinah hired a professional cook who'd come from Seattle too late to find a good claim. Nannie and another woman of her tribe agreed to help serve the food, and with Dinah sharing the work, they managed to feed their customers.

Even with the large amount of food she'd had shipped in, it was obvious that she, too, would be out of food before winter was over, so she started rationing the servings each person could have, and she knew many miners left the table hungry. To supplement her food supply, she hired Jack to bring in several moose and caribou, but even this she served sparingly, for Jack warned that as winter lengthened, game would become scarce.

Knowing that many of the cheechakos had not made a strike, she kept her prices low, intending to make just enough to cover her costs. In some instances, she gave food away to those who were down and out. When she tallied her receipts against expenses, she admitted wryly that she wasn't a good businesswoman.

Near the end of September, when word came that there wouldn't be any more boats in Dawson until spring, the Mounties posted signs: FLEE FOR YOUR LIVES! ALL WHO REMAIN IN DAWSON WITHOUT ADEQUATE FOOD DO SO AT THEIR OWN RISK.

Several hundred men headed downstream after news circulated that food was available at Circle City and Fort Yukon, including Hank Sterling and his partner. Hank stopped at the hotel to see Dinah before he left.

"We don't have enough food to last us, and there's no chance of getting any. If it's a bad winter, we might not be able to work outside much anyway, so we're leaving. Seth and Vance will keep an eye on things until spring."

After Hank left, Dinah wondered again if he could have killed Joseph Morgan. If he felt any guilt, however, he skillfully suppressed it around Seth. But she preferred to suspect Joe Arthur, wryly admitting that was because she didn't like Joe, and she did like Hank. All summer Dinah had dreaded Sam's arrival and his recognition of the assassin, but the Negro hadn't arrived before the freeze-up, so she knew they'd have peace on that score until spring.

Timothy ran into Dinah's office late that same day and said, "Trouble is brewing, and we can't do much about it. Prepare for a riot tonight."

"What do you mean?"

"Most of the cheechakos without supplies have left, but a few of the more lawless ones are roaming the streets in a drunken state, vowing to take what they want from those who have supplies. The miners who have food are standing over their caches, armed to the teeth. Constantine sent me to stay here tonight. Is there anyone else who can handle a gun?"

"The cook and Jack are both here. And, of course, I have a rifle."

"You?" Timothy said.

"Do you think I could have survived this long in the north without knowing how to shoot? My father taught me that as soon as we arrived here."

He shook his head. "You're so beautiful and petite, it surprises me, that's all. I thought you'd need my protection."

"I do, and I'm glad for it, but I can help, also."

As they waited in the darkness, watching the hordes of desperate men stalking the streets, Dinah said, "It doesn't seem right to be guarding our supplies. If we have food, we should share it with those who have none. That's the Christian way."

"Have you ever considered what it would be like to starve to death?" Timothy replied brusquely. "If you give your food to those men, Constantine will drive you out of the city, too. They knew before they arrived that food was scarce, and they had ample warning to leave."

About midnight, six men approached the hotel, shouting and swearing, but when warning shots from four rifles echoed over their heads, they backed away.

As they continued their vigil, streaks of light shattered the darkness, and Dinah could clearly see the Golden Nugget on the opposite side of the street.

"Have the looters set a fire?" she whispered.

Slipping quietly out on the porch, Jack returned, his eyes wide with apprehension. "Lights. In north."

"Why, yes," Timothy said excitedly, "it's the aurora."

With Timothy at her heels, Dinah moved to the porch and looked around her. The whole sky quivered like jelly, and shafts of multicolored lights darted toward the earth. The auroras flickered around them, alternately fading and brightening to display green, red, and purple streaks. In their kennels the malamutes tugged at their chains and howled, to be answered by wolves roaming the mountains around Dawson.

The Athapaskans reacted to the Northern Lights much as

they had to the eclipse of the sun, and even Dinah felt her skin crawl as she viewed the unusual phenomencn.

"I've always heard that such a tremendous display of lights portends a world disaster of some kind. Maybe the United States will go to war with Spain after all," Timothy said, leaving Dinah to wonder if there wasn't a little superstition in every race.

The lights faded gradually, and the night presented no further threat. Timothy seemed to think the danger had passed.

"We have nothing to fear now except a Yukon winter, and that may be more dangerous than a few marauding cheechakos."

By the first of October, large chunks of ice had formed in the river, surrounding the few boats left along the waterfront. In a month, the river froze solid, and Dinah experienced some apprehension when she realized they were isolated in the Klondike. Last year she hadn't minded because she'd been busy on the claim and hardly realized what went on around her, but as she looked at the homesick stampeders who roamed the streets of Dawson, she had a sense of futility.

"Vanity, vanity, all is vanity," Solomon had said more than 2,500 years ago. Solomon was a man who had everything and had done almost everything by his own account, so wouldn't he be an authority on the subject? What then was important? Certainly not the gold men sought, nor the so-called pleasure that fleeting riches brought them. What was the real meaning of life? Solomon had summed it up when he stated that only the person with God in his life possessed a meaningful existence.

Believing that herself, Dinah sought out Father Judge's little mission. Although his religion differed from hers, Dinah respected him as one of the few persons in Dawson dedicated to serving mankind.

The ashen-faced priest had worked continuously since his arrival in Dawson the previous spring, and his efforts had already earned him the nickname the *Saint of Dawson*. The priest had almost single-handedly built a hospital, church, and residences for the staff he hoped to have. He gathered dried grasses from the hill for mattress padding, and he collected herbs to supplement his meager medical supplies. The furniture for his compound consisted of rough boards nailed on stumps. In the church, he substituted white muslin for stained-glass windows, and he carved the altar with a common penknife.

Keeping only a few of the medicines she'd brought from the States, Dinah took the rest with her to the mission. She found the priest huddled beside a cot, holding the emaciated body of a fever victim crying out for relief. Dinah moved to the other side of the cot, and the muscles she'd developed at the mine site and on the Chilkoot Trail stood her in good stead as she helped the priest calm the tormented man. When he lapsed into a coma, the priest nodded his thanks to Dinah and motioned her to follow him from the ward.

She eyed the little hospital, a simple log cabin with a few cubicles to serve as private rooms. Cots ranged around the middle of the main cabin. The hospital housed only a few patients today, but Dinah figured it would bulge with occupants before winter passed.

Leading her into a tiny office, Father Judge asked softly, "And what may I do for you today, Miss?"

With a bright smile, Dinah said, "I came to find out what I can do for you. I don't imagine you're overstaffed here."

"Only three sisters to help me. I've sent word to the Outside for others, but they won't arrive until spring."

"I'm sure that the shortage of food will force me to close my restaurant before the first of the year. I'm not a nurse, but I can assist some way. I'll be available to help you when I'm needed."

"Thank you. I shall depend upon that."

"And I'll give you these medicines. I'm sure your patients will need them before the winter is over."

The priest looked so frail that Dinah questioned if he could possibly live through the winter himself. Before she left the compound, Dinah wandered behind the hospital to see the spring that provided most of the pure water Dawson used. During the summer when the river had become polluted, this spring had been a lifesaver.

Coming suddenly into the glade where the spring gurgled softly into a sunken barrel, Dinah almost stumbled over a nun kneeling in the path. She startled the young woman, who jumped to her feet, tears covering her face. The anguished look in the girl's eyes surprised Dinah, for the nuns she'd known had always been serene of countenance.

Surmising that the girl was even younger than herself, Dinah put an arm around her. "My dear, what's your trouble? I'll be glad to listen. I'm Dinah Davis."

"Please forget you saw me in tears. I must return now before Sister Anne misses me." She forced a wan smile to her lips and wiped her eyes. "Thank you."

"What's your name?"

"In another life, I was Gail Sandover. Here, I'm Sister Phoebe."

"If you ever need help, come to me."

"You've never been in orders, Miss. We don't make our own decisions," she said bitterly.

Dinah watched the retreating girl's back, wondering what had caused her tears.

Within six weeks, Dinah fed only charity cases, and when Seth and Vance came to town to check on her, Seth scolded her soundly.

"But Dinah, you can't afford to do that!"

"And why not? These men came to Dawson too late to make a gold strike. They don't have the money to pay high prices for their food. I'll share what I have as long as I can; then I'll close the restaurant until spring. I can't turn people away when I have that big bank account in Portland, and I'm assuming you've found some more gold for me."

"Not yet, but we have our equipment in place."

"What about your claim, Vance?"

"It's working out about a hundred dollars to a pan, and Seth says that's good."

"How do you like being a miner?"

"I've found it isn't easy, and I don't really care that much about the gold. Since my family has always had plenty of money, I don't crave gold like some people do, but I do like the feeling of accomplishment. I've never really *had* to work, so it's good to find that I can do something successfully."

"The two of you should come in for Christmas, and invite Waldo and Susie, too. I'm going to have a big dinner for my customers, and then I'll close until a supply boat arrives after the thaw."

"I don't celebrate Christmas," Seth said, "but I'll send Vance in. It isn't safe for us to leave the claim unattended. We brought the dogs with us, or we both wouldn't be here now."

"I can keep them here," Dinah said. "I don't want anyone to steal those dogs. We may need them before the winter is over."

"It hasn't come to that yet, although it may. Right now they're safer at the mine," Seth said. "Have you had any trouble? I didn't know about the rioting here in Dawson until a few days ago."

"Oh, we had no problem at all. Corporal McCormick came and spent the night here, and of course, Jack was around. We were safe enough."

"Who's McCormick?"

"He's a Mountie I met at Fortymile last summer. He's been friendly to me since then."

Could that be jealousy mirrored on Seth's face? *Too much to hope for*, Dinah thought as Seth said calmly, "It's always good to have friends in the right places."

"I'm concerned about the spiritual welfare of these miners, Seth. Many of them are God-fearing people, and they don't have anyplace to loaf except the saloons. I think someone should conduct Sunday services for them."

"William Judge can give them all the spiritual help they need."

"That poor man is overworked now. You're a preacher. Why don't you do it?"

"I'm not a preacher, so forget it."

"Then I'll do it myself."

"Go ahead! You seem intent on doing everything else that only men should do."

He left the room, and Dinah dropped into a chair with a sigh. Vance laughed and said, "You two can't be together ten minutes until the sparks fly. Seth has been worrying ever since you moved to Dawson, fretting about you being here alone, and you were obviously delighted to see him. You like each other, so why do you quarrel?"

"I really don't know. I make up my mind not to argue with him, and the first thing I know, we're at it again."

From where she sat, Dinah observed Seth going into the Golden Nugget. After Vance went to a room, Dinah watched the door of the saloon for more than an hour, but Seth didn't come out. She knew he didn't drink or gamble, so why was he staying there so long? Her mind refused to accept the logical answer.

After the first of the year, Dinah closed her restaurant, but she kept the hotel available to anyone who needed a room, whether or not he could pay. The Indians went back to the village, and Susie came into Dawson to spend the winter months with Dinah, asserting that Dinah needed a chaperon.

"Waldo's getting restless again," she told Dinah on their first night together. "It was his idea for me to come here to Dawson. He wanted to be alone. He's moody, and something's bothering him. I can't figure him out."

"Maybe he'll come in and have services here at the hotel for the miners. I can't supply them any physical food, but at least they can be fed spiritually. I've been singing with them and reading the Bible, but they'd probably like to hear a sermon."

"I talked to him about that, but he refused."

"Actually, what do you know about Waldo?"

"Not a thing more than what you know. He's been a good husband, as far as husbands go, but his past is a mystery to me. Of course, I've never thought much about it, because most of the people who emigrated to Oregon came because they wanted to leave their pasts behind them, including your own relatives."

"Since he is a preacher, I didn't think you'd have any need to worry."

"I don't suppose I do have anything to worry about, but he acts like a man with something to hide, and I want to know what it is. I have to caution myself to let sleeping dogs lie. He dodges out of sight if anyone strange comes around the claim, and sometimes in his sleep, he'll call out, 'There's a step on my trail.' " Susie shook her head. "Be careful whom you marry, Dinah."

Laughing, Dinah said, "I sometimes wonder if I'll ever be married."

"With all the men in this gold town, I'd think you would have lots of offers."

"I have, but I'm never sure who wants me or who wants my gold, so I've elected to stay single."

"That Mountie seems mighty interested in you."

"He's a fine man," Dinah agreed, but she knew that Timothy would never be fine enough to replace Seth in her heart. It would have to be Seth or nobody, and at the rate they were going, it would never be Seth.

As the food supply declined, illness increased. Men caught a few fish by cutting holes in the thick ice of the creeks, and an occasional moose or caribou ventured into town looking for food, only to be shot by a desperate miner hungrier than the animals. The people ate enough to keep them alive, but not enough to keep them well.

By the last of February, Father Judge had forty-five scurvy patients, and as Dinah worked daily in the hospital, she learned the horrors of the dreadful disease preying upon any population that went too long without fresh food. It took all the courage she had to sit beside a scurvy victim who vomited blood and his teeth at the same time. She watched helplessly as dark green and ugly black spots marred a man's skin until he hemorrhaged to death.

Medical supplies diminished, and the nuns allotted medication sparingly, hoping to have it last through the winter. Dinah brought the last remaining drugs she had to supplement their meager store.

The temperature rose to zero by mid-March, and Dinah watched the lengthening daylight hours with optimism, thinking that the winter had done its worst. But that was before Vance appeared at the hotel one snowy day.

He came to the point immediately. "Seth is real sick. I've done all I can for him, and I thought maybe you or Susie could come to the claim and help. He hasn't been out of bed for a week."

Dinah jumped out of her chair as if she'd been stung. "I'll go."

Bundling into a heavy hooded parka and donning sealskin mukluks, she wrapped a few biscuits and some roasted moose meat in a bundle. "We'll stop by the hospital to see if Father Judge has any medicine I can take along."

The nuns could spare only a few spoonfuls of dried herbs.

"I'm sorry, my daughter, that we have nothing more," Father Judge said. "I left a large cache of opium and pare-goric, as well as headache powders, at Circle City. If we could find someone to go after that, the lives of many people might be saved."

"Of course, they may have been found and used by now."

He smiled slightly. "I think not, unless they tore down my cabin."

Dinah hastily took the trail for Eldorado Creek, traveling so rapidly that Vance finally stopped and called to her. "I can't keep up this pace, and I don't think you can, either. Seth isn't going to die before we get there. I'm slowing down; you can do what you want to."

"Sorry, Vance," Dinah said as she slowed to a moderate gait. "I'm worried about him."

"So am I, but I don't intend to collapse from exhaustion before we reach the cabin."

Seth burned with fever and had lost so much weight that she hardly recognized him. He hadn't shaved during the winter, and the dark whiskers accentuated the hollowness of his eyes and bony cheeks.

"Oh, Seth," she whispered, tears in her eyes as she dropped beside his cot and put her arms around him.

"Better stay away from me," he whispered weakly. "I don't know what's the matter."

Turning to Vance, she asked, "What about your diet?"

"Seth hasn't been able to eat anything for a week, but we've had plenty of food, and still have lime and lemon juice that we drink every morning. But we had a miner stop and stay the night here two weeks ago. He was sick, and I think Seth caught whatever he had."

"If you've had good food, you don't have scurvy. I've

learned quite a lot about nursing in the past few months, and I imagine you have a bad case of the ague. Have you vomited and had diarrhea?"

Seth nodded. "And fever, too."

"I'll see what I can do."

But after two days and nights of dosing him with the herbs she'd brought and trying to feed him nourishing broths, Seth seemed even worse than when she'd come. She came to a swift decision.

"He has to have some medication, and I'm going after it."

"But there isn't any medicine," Vance said.

"Not in Dawson, but there's some in Circle City. If not there, then I'll go to Fort Yukon. He isn't going to die if I can do anything about it."

"No, Dinah," Seth protested from his cot. "Get somebody else to go."

"Anyone who can handle a dog team is either too sick to go or out on his claim. I'll stop at the Indian camp and ask Jack to go with me."

Before she went to the kennels to harness the dogs, she bent over and kissed Seth on the forehead. He grasped her hand tightly and murmured, "Be careful."

"Pray for my safety, Seth," she said, but he turned his head away.

The malamutes hadn't been worked for weeks, and they were so excited at the chance to take a run that Dinah could hardly hold them until she stepped on the sled. They yelped and jumped in their harnesses, and when she released the brake, the three dogs shot out of the camp with a speed that took her breath.

Entering the streets of Dawson, she went first to the hospital to see Father Judge.

"I'm going to Circle to get those drugs, if you'll tell me where they are."

The priest stared at her for a moment from his cadaverous eyes, but he didn't try to dissuade her.

"In the north wall, about three feet from the rear door, you will find a hollow log lying next to the ceiling. I carved a hiding place there. Remove the carefully concealed slab to find the entrance. There are several bags of medicines that I couldn't haul when I came here last spring."

"I'll find them. Pray for me."

"God's blessings go with you, my daughter."

Next she stopped at the hotel, and during the spate of Susie's protests, she put on a pair of sealskin pants and a woolen shirt that a miner had given her in payment for his week's lodging. Over her parka, she donned a cotton windbreaker, and then added a pair of fur-lined gloves.

The trail to the Indian village wound through timber, but she followed it easily, reaching it before dark. The silence in the village stunned her, and she called several times before she roused anyone.

Finally, Nannie staggered from their dwelling. "Go away. All sick here. Big sickness."

"But I want Jack to go with me to Circle!" Dinah said fearfully. "You mean he's sick, too?"

"All sick. But we get better soon. We finally caught the *nahani* who brought all this trouble on us." She motioned toward a small hut at the edge of the village. "Pen him up in there. When he dies, the Indians will recover." She staggered back inside the hut.

Dinah turned away with a sinking heart. She had counted so much on Jack's help, and she'd expected to spend the night in the village. But she couldn't take a chance on catching their malady, so she kept her distance from the cabin where the *nahani* lived and traveled several miles down the Yukon to make camp in the open.

Building a small fire, she thawed some meat for the dogs and fed them before she ate anything herself. Then, spreading a tarp on the ground, she gathered the dogs around her, spread another tarp over them, and went to sleep.

The rest of the journey passed in a haze. She followed the Yukon as much as possible to keep from losing her way. At times, she drove the dogs in the face of a thirty-mile-an-hour wind. Another day, a blizzard descended upon her, and the blowing snow made it almost impossible to dodge the large ice chunks on the frozen river.

One night she found an abandoned log cabin which housed her and the dogs. She moved on relentlessly, urged by the fear that Seth would die if he didn't have medicine. Some days she figured she averaged thirty miles, but other days, when the temperature plummeted and the dogs began to stiffen, she spent most of the day seeing to their comfort.

Generally the dogs cooperated, although on one occasion they erupted into a terrible fight, snarling at one another and tearing at one another's throats. Following the example Jack had taught her, she grabbed the whip and waded into their midst, beating them until they settled down.

Once the wind upended the sled, and she had to reload her gear. When the dogs wearied, she ran behind the sled to lighten their burden.

Ten days after she left Dawson, Dinah entered the streets of Circle City. She expected to find the town deserted, but pulling up before a lighted saloon, she entered to find a crowded building.

"Will somebody tend to my dogs, please, and give me a cup of hot coffee?"

Looking round, she recognized Hank Sterling and some of the other miners who had fled Dawson earlier in the year. They crowded around her, and Hank helped her remove the heavy outer garments and ordered two men to take care of the malamutes. Now that she'd reached the safety of the town, her body shook until her teeth chattered. She bit her lips to keep from crying.

"Is anyone living in our cabin?" she asked the bartender, who'd been in Circle City when she'd lived there.

"No, Miss Dinah, but you'd better sleep here tonight where it's warm. What brought you to Circle?"

"There's a lot of sickness in Dawson, and I came to get some supplies Father Judge left here."

"You don't mean you came by yourself?" Hank asked.

At her nod, he said, "Well, you won't go back alone. I'll take you."

Sensing the need to hurry, Dinah rested only one day before she set out again. In addition to the drugs the priest had stashed, she also ransacked her cabin and Susie's for a few cans of provisions to pack on the sled.

As she and Hank ran down the street behind the sled and out on the frozen Yukon, the shouts of an encouraging crowd followed them. With Hank's help, the return trip should go quickly.

Chapter Ten

Winter–Spring 1898

*E*ven with Hank to help and keep her company, the return to Dawson dragged interminably. What if Seth died before she arrived with the medicine? The thought haunted Dinah until she could hardly stop to rest the dogs or herself, but she knew she had to conserve the animals.

The temperature had moderated considerably by the time they arrived at Dawson, and since it was midday, Dinah stopped only long enough to leave most of the medicines with Father Judge and see Susie before she headed toward Bonanza Creek.

Giving her a generous portion of the headache medicine but a scant quantity of opium, Judge cautioned, "Careful with this powder, Dinah. It's a great drug for pain and diarrhea, but it can become addictive."

Vance rushed to greet her when she halted before the cabin.

"How is he?"

"No better, but he's still hanging on. I haven't worked any

since you left, fearing to leave him alone. He's fretted constantly about you."

She turned the dogs into the kennel, leaving them in their harnesses, and hurried into the cabin.

Hollow-eyed and gaunt, Seth watched from his cot. Dropping to her knees beside him, she reached for his hand. Now that she knew she had come in time to save his life, her body trembled.

"Are you all right?" he whispered weakly, his eyes eagerly searching her face.

"I'm fine, and I've brought medicine for you."

Dinah put slabs of salmon on the stove to thaw for the dogs, then she opened a can of peaches she'd brought from Circle and poured some of the juice into a cup. With a spoon, she slowly fed Seth a good portion of the juice and gave him some medicine. She washed his face with a warm cloth and plumped his pillow.

"I'm going to kennel the dogs and feed them, and by that time, we should know if you're going to retain the juice and medicine. Then I'll use Vance's cot for a long rest."

"But how . . . ?" he began.

Dinah put her fingers on his parched lips. "No questions now. I'm here, and all is fine. We'll talk when you're feeling better."

His meek assent to her suggestion brought tears to Dinah's eyes. How she wished he was strong enough to quarrel with her again! She hurried out of the cabin before he could see her emotion, silently breathing a prayer of thanks that God had brought her safely through the difficult journey.

Dinah waited until the dogs had satisfied their hunger, then she removed gobs of ice and sticks from their fur. She brushed their coats, checking carefully for any wounds. She applied ointment to the raw spots where the harnesses had galled them and to the cuts on their feet caused by jagged ice tufts.

"Thank you, my friends," she murmured aloud to the dogs. "If it weren't for your faithfulness, I couldn't have made it."

They nuzzled her face and rubbed against her legs as she continued to minister to them. As she worked, she wondered if Seth would ever admit that she'd probably saved his life because she hadn't followed his advice to be a "lady."

Within a week Seth's health had improved until he could resume a solid diet, and Dinah searched through their provisions to find foods to tempt his appetite. The day he felt able to sit at the table for his meals was a time of celebration. Dinah baked a dried-apple pie to go with the pan of moose stew she'd prepared.

As she watched the way Vance wolfed the meal, she said, "Have you men done any cooking at all this winter?"

"We've tried," Vance admitted with a sheepish grin, "but neither of us is a very good cook."

"No wonder you're sick, Seth. From the sizable supply of foodstuffs you have left, I figured you hadn't eaten much."

With Dinah there to look after Seth, Vance started working his claim again, which left Seth and Dinah alone many hours. Much of the time, he slept. But one day, after he'd silently watched her move around the cabin sifting gold from the sand Vance had brought the day before, he said, "Dinah, when you've finished that, I want to talk to you."

A tone in his voice that she hadn't heard before alerted Dinah to the fact that their relationship might have entered a new phase. Willing herself to finish the work without hurrying—it was a slow job, anyway—she didn't go to him for almost an hour. Seth took her hand and pulled her to a seat beside him on the cot.

"Dinah, I love you," he said without preliminaries. She caught her breath in a half sob. What she'd wanted for two years had finally come when she'd least expected it.

"I realized that after you left for Circle City, and I didn't have a peaceful moment while you were gone. I suppose I've loved you right from the first, and that's why I tried to make a lady out of you." He smiled slightly at his memories. "From the first day I saw you, I felt close to you, and I wanted to protect you, almost as if you were a sister."

"Seth, I don't want to be treated like a sister. I love you, too. I've known it since that day in Circle City when you shook me."

"The first time I thought of you as a desirable woman was that day I followed you up the Chilkoot Trail dressed in those bloomers. Although I was so mad, I'd gladly have strangled you, I couldn't be indifferent to your charm."

He pulled Dinah down and kissed her, and a surge of emotion engulfed Dinah. Her body responded to Seth's caresses until she felt as if the exalted music of a great orchestra tuned her passions to his. *So this is what it means to love a man.*

She realized that Seth's reactions must rival hers, for he abruptly pulled away. Though he released her lips, he still held her in his arms.

"I've been a fool," he said remorsefully.

She wondered if he referred to his relationship with Dixie Belle. How was she going to deal with that situation? Ignore it, as she had for the past year?

"Have you accepted the fact that I'll never act as a lady?"

He smiled wryly. "I realize now that being a lady includes more than adhering to social mores. I'll admit that I might not be living today if you hadn't known how to handle that team of dogs. We'll have to accept each other as we are."

He caressed her hair, but he seemed deep in thought, so Dinah didn't speak, content for the moment to rest in his arms and to know that he cared for her. Her heart plummeted at his next words.

"But I can't ask you to marry me yet. Two things have to be straightened out in my life. You asked me to pray for your safety, and I did. That's the first time I've been able to com-

municate with God for years. During my illness I've had time
to assess my spiritual condition. I've sinned against God,
and I've asked Him to forgive me and restore the zeal to
serve Him that I had in my youth."

" 'If we confess our sins, he is faithful and just to forgive
us our sins, and to cleanse us from all unrighteousness.' "

"I know, Dinah. I've said those words over and over, but
I have something to renounce before I can receive full for-
giveness."

Did he refer to his relationship with Dixie Belle?

"I still can't forget the desire to avenge my father's death.
When Sam arrives, I think he'll be able to identify the person
who killed Dad, if he's here in the Klondike. If I find out who
the man is, perhaps I can forgive him. It's not knowing that
bothers me."

"But thousands of people will arrive here before the summer is over. It will be a miracle if you ever know who did the
killing. It's been so long. How can it matter now?"

"It shouldn't matter, but it does."

" 'But if ye forgive not men their trespasses, neither will
your Father forgive your trespasses.' You know those words
as well as I do. Unless you forget this silly vengeance of
yours, God can't forgive you."

He kissed her again. "I refuse to start arguing with you
today."

"Do you mean we won't quarrel again?"

"Don't count on that. I just won't quarrel with you today."

As much as she loved him, Dinah knew that Seth's avenging spirit and his association with Dixie Belle stood in the
way of happiness. She'd watched Seth go into the Golden
Nugget every time he had come to Dawson, and he had to be
going to see Dixie. Although she hadn't mentioned the
woman to him today, she knew she'd have to before she
could possibly agree to become his wife.

By the end of April, Seth was at last able to go back to

work, and Dinah prepared to leave for Dawson. Compared with last year, spring came quite early. With eighteen hours of sunshine, the temperature rose to over ninety degrees on some days. Snow vanished from the mountains overnight. Small streams gurgled through the dense underbrush and spewed into the Bonanza, overflowing layers of ice.

"Fine weather for mining gold," Waldo commented when he stopped by after a trip to Dawson. "Miners up and down the creeks are busily shoveling pay dirt from the winter's dump into sluice boxes and funneling water through them to wash out the gold. Lots of men are finding their months of hard work have paid off."

"Now that I'm on my feet again, Vance and I want to start that tomorrow."

"When are you going back to Dawson, Dinah?" Waldo asked.

"Soon. These men don't need me now."

"The townspeople are surely excited. Water is running over the top of the ice in the Yukon, and the ice is pushing upward, causing water to overflow the lowlands. The Indians say the flats where Dawson is located flooded so much several years ago that they rowed their boats across the area. Constantine is right anxious about it."

"I'd better return tomorrow, if that's the case. I'll need to protect my property, and I'll send Susie home if it floods."

"Then, too," Waldo continued, "news keeps creeping in about thousands of cheechakos on their way to the Klondike."

"How is the news coming in if the river is still frozen?" Seth asked.

"A few stampeders have sledded their outfits down the river. One man brought in two-hundred-dozen eggs, which he sold in less than an hour for thirty-six-hundred dollars. The newcomers say that thousands of people are waiting on this side of Chilkoot and White passes to enter Dawson as soon as the breakup occurs."

Waldo's words excited Dinah, and she prepared to leave the next morning. Seth waited until Vance vacated the cabin, then he hugged Dinah to him. Even as he held her close in his arms, she found it hard to believe that he loved her.

"Dinah, I'm going to miss you, but it's a good thing you're returning to Dawson. Until we're married, we can't handle much more of this togetherness, if you know what I mean."

Dinah knew what he meant. In spite of Vance's presence in the cabin, she'd been hard put to keep her hands away from Seth. Even Vance must have sensed the tension build up between them, because he observed them wonderingly from time to time, obviously puzzled at the change in their relationship.

Yes, she must leave, but now that she knew Seth loved her, Dinah dreaded the separation.

Dinah went first to the Mounties' headquarters. Finding Timothy and Constantine in the office, she asked, "What are the dangers of flooding? Should I move my fixtures to the second floor?"

"You should have stayed at the claim, Miss," Constantine said brusquely. "We may have to evacuate this town."

"I have quite an investment in Dawson. You can't expect me to allow it to be flooded without my being here. Besides, I heard there are many people on their way, and I want my hotel open to house them."

"At this point," Timothy said, "the water is still two feet below the top of the bank. Wait until the ice breakup before you do anything."

Two days later, Dinah awakened to a crackling roar, and she knew the ice had broken. Throwing on some clothes, she rushed to Front Street, where it seemed the whole of Dawson watched the flowing river. The ice had parted in the middle, and the swift current jostled huge ice masses, while water played like fountains around the jagged blocks. Chunks of frozen snow and ice piled up along Front Street, and in the curve of the river, ice jams narrowed the channel.

Dinah watched in fascination as the river that had been ice-bound for months raced in freedom toward the Bering Sea.

"Cheechako!" someone shouted, and looking upstream, Dinah saw a small boat dodging in and out of the ice blocks, jostling for a safe landing along the shore. Dinah wasn't as much interested in the new arrival as she was the muddy river inching closer to the town.

Meeting Constantine as she walked back to the hotel, she said, "I'd better clear the furniture out of the downstairs, don't you think?"

Grimly, he nodded. Dinah had no trouble finding men to help her. Many of last fall's arrivals hadn't staked claims, and they'd roamed the streets of Dawson for months. Most of them were destitute. Dinah had brought back some meal and flour from Seth's supplies, and when she offered her workers a home-cooked meal, she had more help than she actually needed. They soon cleared the main floor of the hotel, except for the stove, which could easily be moved when the water started in the door. She settled down to wait.

Dinah had brought two of her dogs into Dawson when she came from the mine, and she needed to get them out of town before the flood came. She didn't want to leave, and she didn't trust her dogs to everyone. When she heard of a sledder heading toward Fort Yukon, she asked him to take a message to the Athapaskan village. If the Crows had survived the winter, Jack would help her. When Jack and Nannie arrived a week later, water loomed closer to her hotel.

Shaking hands gravely with the two friends, who looked gaunt and emaciated, Dinah said, "You must have had a bad winter."

"Much sick," Nannie said. "But we kept the *nahani* locked up. He's sick, too. Took our sickness and put on him."

"You still have him imprisoned?"

"Yes," Jack said, "but no need to, now. He's too sick to get away."

"Jack, will you take my dogs to the claim and leave them with Seth? I don't want them here when the water comes."

After Jack left, Nannie and Dinah went to the spring behind the hospital and carried several jugs of water to the second floor of the hotel.

They encountered Sister Phoebe at the spring, and she watched the freedom of their movements with envy. Dinah had visited with the young woman often during the winter, and on one of her despondent days, Phoebe had confided to Dinah, "Sometimes I feel like a prisoner, and I long to escape. Is it wrong to desire a family of my own? I was too young to make such a serious decision when I became a novice."

Now that Dinah knew the cause of Phoebe's unhappiness, she longed to help her, but what could she do?

In preparation for the expected flood, they also baked loaves of bread and cooked other food they could store without spoiling.

"We may be anticipating a crisis that won't come, but it's best to be prepared," Dinah reasoned.

When Jack returned from the claim, Seth came with him. "I wanted to see how things are here. We keep hearing horror stories about the situation in Dawson."

"The Mounties say we're bound to have a flood, but perhaps it won't get inside my building. That's the reason I built the first floor several feet above ground."

"Seems like a lot of excitement in town. Have many new people come in?"

"The ones who wintered between here and Lake Bennett have arrived, but the main stampede is yet to come. Timothy told me that the Mounties have already checked three thousand boats through Lake Tagish, and more arrive every hour."

"I couldn't believe it when I saw a crate of chickens at the police barracks. After the trip we had over the Chilkoot, I find it hard to believe a man could make it with a crate of live chickens on his sled."

"And when I considered how much trouble I had bringing Bathsheba from Circle City, I was amazed when a man brought in a scowload of kittens. He sold them quickly to lonesome miners who wanted something for company."

Pointing to her Gibson Girl dress, Nannie said, "Look!"

"Oh, yes," Dinah said, "one man brought in some dresses and bonnets. I'd bought so many things in Portland last summer that I didn't buy anything for myself, but I thought Nannie deserved a new dress."

"If you're sure you'll be all right, I'll head back to the claim," Seth said the next morning, as he anxiously eyed the several inches of water covering the street in front of the hotel.

"If you don't go now, you might be stuck here for days," Dinah said. "And I'll get along fine with Jack and Nannie for company. We'll be comfortable on the second floor, and if the water rises any higher than that, we can leave by boat or go to the third floor."

"Dinah, I'm miserable away from you," Seth said, drawing her into a tight embrace for a good-bye kiss. "I want to be married now, but it wouldn't be fair to you until I can straighten out my life."

Nuzzling her head under his chin, Dinah said, "Maybe it won't be long, Seth."

In a few days, five feet of water covered most of Dawson's business section. Jack had secured a boat to a post on the front porch, and when the water started to recede, Nannie and Dinah walked through the water and climbed in the boat. Jack took them on a tour of the town, rowing slowly along Front Street where cabin roofs protruded from the muddy water. Dixie Belle and Mary Lou waved from the second floor of the Golden Nugget, and a few other people peered from windows, but for the most part, the town appeared deserted.

"Much mud to clean up when this water goes down," Nannie commented as they waded back into the hotel.

"I'll hire workers to sweep the mud from the floor as the water leaves. I don't know what they'll do about mud on the streets."

By June fifth, the water had receded, and three days later, cheechakos descended on Dawson. Men poured in day and night without a break. Space along the shoreline was soon crowded, and later arrivals tied their crafts to other boats and leaped from boat to boat to reach shore.

Patrons filled Dinah's hotel as soon as the floor dried and she moved her furniture back in place. Most of the new arrivals, however, simply hoisted their tents on the hilltops overlooking the town and along the trails that led to the gold fields.

Although the full hotel kept all of them busy, Dinah took time to range up and down the creeks raising money for Father Judge's church. After the painstaking work he'd done on the original building, it had been destroyed by fire on Trinity Sunday. Nothing was saved, and when the priest, without complaint, started to rebuild, Dinah did what she could to help him.

When Alex McDonald volunteered to pay for the cost of the chapel, Dinah and other women donated the funds they'd collected to complete the building of the hospital. With the influx of cheechakos, sickness had accelerated, and the expanded hospital became a necessity.

"I'm worried about the health of these people now," Constantine mentioned one night when he and Timothy stopped by the hotel for dinner. "Too many of them don't observe any sanitation rules. They're walking in slime up to their ankles, and after they've thrown their trash in the river, they use the water for their personal needs."

"We're starting a campaign to clean up everything, but it will take time," Timothy said.

Father Judge's hospital filled rapidly with typhoid and scurvy victims, and Dinah spent as much time as possible helping the overworked nuns. She gained a new respect for Phoebe, who admittedly was unhappy with her lot yet worked long hours without complaint.

One morning when Dinah went to the hospital, she found Dixie Belle lying among the men in the main ward. The girl's head moved restlessly on the grass-filled pillow.

Phoebe was clearing Father Judge's own room to make a place for the woman, and Dinah said impulsively, "Why don't I take her to the hotel and care for her?"

"That will be rather hard on your business, won't it?" Father Judge said.

"I'll house her in a room on the third floor, and I'll leave the hotel work up to Nannie and the others. In spite of her profession, I hate to see her die here. She is dying, isn't she?"

"Only God knows," Judge answered, "but she's been sick for several days. Her friends couldn't do anything more for her."

Dinah found four men to carry Dixie to the hotel, and when she started to follow, Father Judge put his hand on her shoulder. "You have a heart of gold, my daughter."

The priest occasionally sent Phoebe to spell Dinah from Dixie's bedside, and Phoebe was there one day when Vance came in. In the privacy of the sickroom, the nun had laid aside her veil. "Well, I say!" he stammered. "Why haven't I seen you before?" Vance's eyes roamed over the girl's face, and he breathed deeply, as if he'd seen a miracle.

Phoebe's face colored as she dropped her eyes from Vance's admiring gaze.

Thinking it wise to forestall Vance's ardor before it progressed further, Dinah said, "Vance, this is *Sister* Phoebe."

Engrossed as he was in the girl's beauty, he still didn't tumble to Phoebe's profession until she reached for her veil and planted it firmly on her head.

"Oh," he said, as he suddenly resembled a punctured balloon.

"Good-bye, Dinah. I'll be back tomorrow," Phoebe said as she rushed by Vance and headed downstairs.

Vance stared after her as one in a trance, and Dinah thought it better not to comment upon his enchantment. She drew Vance into the hallway and said, "I think Dixie is dying, and you'd better tell Seth about her when you return to the mine. I don't know how he's involved with her, but I suppose he should be told about her illness."

When Seth rushed into the room the next day, his face pale, a bleak look in his eyes, Dinah went out and closed the door, leaving them together. Dixie was having one of her lucid moments, and Dinah didn't want to know what they said to each other.

Seth took a room in the hotel, seemingly with no notion of returning to the claim. He helped Dinah with the care of the woman, leaving Phoebe to give more attention to her hospital duties.

One day when Seth wasn't in the room, Dixie awakened and said to Dinah, "Do you know that I'm Seth's sister?"

The look on Dinah's face must have given Dixie her answer, for she smiled slightly. "I thought he probably hadn't told you. He's ashamed of me, and I suppose he has a right to be."

"So you're Janice Sue," Dinah said wonderingly, realizing now that Seth hadn't mentioned her name since they'd met Dixie on the Chilkoot Trail.

"I just couldn't stick it out at home after Seth left. Unless you've lived there, you can't realize how depressing it was in the postwar South. Everybody lived in the past, hating the Yankees, talking about what life used to be. Nobody had any optimism. I stood it as long as I could, and I ran away with a man who promised to marry me. When he wouldn't, I didn't have any choice except to turn to the life I'm living. I didn't know how to do anything else. I'd been taught to live as a Southern belle had lived before the war, and my only accomplishment was the art of being pleasant to men so I could win a rich husband. Unfortunately, there were few rich men after eighteen sixty-five."

"When did Seth know about this?"

"Not until he saw me along the Chilkoot Trail. That's the reason he asked Joe's party to travel with him. He tried to make me turn back, but when I wouldn't, he felt responsible for me."

"Thank you for telling me," Dinah said softly.

"You don't know how much I've admired you, Dinah. You're what I'd like to have been, but I didn't have the courage. Try to make it up to Seth for the way I turned out. I've hurt him, but you can make him happy. He told me that he loves you."

Those were the last words Dixie spoke, and she died two days later. Seth knelt beside her bed and wept when it was over.

Dinah touched his shoulder. "She told me she was your sister, Seth. I'm sorry it turned out this way."

He put out his arm and drew Dinah close, his face still lowered on the cot. "I'd rather see her dead than to have her live the life she's been living, but how am I going to tell my mother?"

Chapter Eleven

Summer 1898

*I*n spite of her concern over the illness and subsequent death of Dixie, Dinah had been conscious of Vance's frequent visits to the hotel when Phoebe helped with the nursing. She realized a problem existed, but exhausted as she was with her hotel business and the extra burden of Dixie, Dinah delayed grappling with the difficult situation. But after Dixie's death, Vance came to her.

"You'll have to help me. I can't think of any way to see Phoebe now."

"See Phoebe! You're only making trouble for yourself and her."

"I don't see why! Phoebe is still a novice. It wasn't her idea to become a nun. Her parents died when she was fourteen, and an uncle forced her to take this step. She hasn't made her final vows."

"What do you expect me to do?"

"She'd leave the hospital if she had some place to go. If you offer her a home, that would make it easier for her."

Although Dinah promised Vance she'd talk to the girl, she wondered if the couple realized the problems they faced. But when she went to the hospital the next day, she asked Phoebe to take a walk with her. They climbed the hill behind the hospital, and finding a dry spot under a spruce tree, Dinah invited Phoebe to sit beside her on the brown needles. The fragrant scent of evergreen trees reminded Dinah of the forest near her childhood home in Oregon.

Looking at Phoebe's heart-shaped face, fair skin, and trusting green eyes framed by the dark gray habit she wore, Dinah understood the appeal the girl presented to Vance. In her opinion, Phoebe would make a better mother than she did a nun, but that decision must be made by Phoebe.

"Vance tells me that you've considered forsaking your vows."

Phoebe hid her face in her hands. "Oh, it sounds terrible when you say it! I don't know what to do. I like working with the patients, and I did promise to serve God in this manner. I didn't want to, but there didn't seem to be anything else I could do at the time. I was so young, and no one wanted me."

Dinah contrasted this girl to herself when she lost her parents. She hadn't considered clinging to others when Nelson Davis disappeared, but in similar circumstances Phoebe had been helpless. Dinah wondered if this wasn't what had captivated Vance. Did men prefer weak women? Thinking back to her quarrelsome beginnings with Seth, she knew that this was the type of woman he'd expected her to be. Ha! Not even for Seth would she be a clinging vine.

"Well, you must make up your mind," she told Phoebe bluntly. "Vance thinks you're in love with him. You can't have him and remain faithful to your vows."

"I do love him, and I'd like to marry and have a family. But Sister Anne is the same as a mother to me, and I don't want to disappoint her or Father Judge. Most of the time I like the well-ordered life of a sister."

"You can't have both," Dinah repeated, "and only you can make that decision. If you want to leave the hospital, you can live with me at the hotel. In all fairness to Vance, I think you should make up your mind soon."

Dinah returned to the hotel, somewhat irritated that Vance had involved her in the situation. She wasn't much older than Vance and Phoebe, but sometimes she felt as old as Methuselah. How could she resolve another couple's love affairs when she wasn't doing so well with her own? Perhaps realizing the danger of allowing their emotions to continue unchecked, Seth again treated her as a younger sister. The only difference in their relationship was that they seldom quarreled, although at times Dinah longed for a stimulating battle of words. She supposed she'd have to live with his reticence until he renounced the idea of avenging his father's death.

"Dinah," Jack Crow said, his face more solemn than usual, "I think I have found your father."

Dinah stared at the Indian, amazement on her face. It had been almost two years since her father's disappearance, and she didn't know when she'd finally stopped believing that he lived, but she had.

"He is the *nahani* who has plagued our tribe for so many months. I saw him yesterday, and I'm sure he is your father. He whispers your name."

"Where is he?"

"In his hut in the forest. We have kept him apart from the rest of us for months to ward off his evil influence. Now he is very sick, and I looked in the window yesterday. He calls your name, and I think it is your father."

"I'll come at once, but I want Seth to go with me. We must go to the mine first."

The twenty miles to Eldorado Creek seemed endless, although Dinah and Jack kept a rapid pace. She rushed breathlessly toward Vance and Seth at the entrance of the mine's shaft. For a moment, she couldn't speak, and Seth put his arms around her.

"What is it?"

"Jack thinks the *nahani* we've heard about for so long is Dad," she gasped. "He's very sick now and calling my name. Will you go with me to see him?"

"Of course. Vance, carry on the best you can until we return. I'll stop by the cabin and make a pack; we may be gone several days."

While Seth gathered the supplies, Vance sidled over to Dinah, who had dropped on the ground to rest.

"Have you talked to her?"

"Yes, and I've offered her sanctuary if she wants to leave the hospital. But, Vance, don't pressure the girl. I'm not sure she's ready to forsake her vows. And you be sure she's what you want before you ask it of her. That's a serious decision to make."

"I don't know why she couldn't marry me and still live a worthwhile life."

"Probably she could, but you allow her to decide. You don't want a wife with a guilty conscience."

Jack led the way across country, and when the trail permitted, Seth and Dinah walked side by side.

"I can't understand this, Seth. Why did Dad desert me?"

"I don't believe he deserted you. Something happened to make him forget who he was. Maybe he fell and injured himself."

"If only he'd allowed me to go prospecting with him, as I begged him to," Dinah moaned. "But he didn't think it was fitting for a woman," she added dismally. "If I'd been with him, I could have found help when he was hurt."

When they reached the small hut in the woods, Jack motioned Dinah to enter. She retched at the putrid smell in the place as she knelt to look closely at the man lying on a pile of grass and skins. His hair was long and matted. Whiskers covered his face. Strands of hide and vines held his ragged clothes together. Nothing about this human skeleton reminded Dinah of her father.

She looked at Seth, whose face showed concern and disbelief. Seeing the question in her eyes, Seth pointed to the back of the man's hand. A long pink scar blazed vividly against the grayish skin. It was Nelson Davis, all right: That was the scar he'd gotten a few weeks before he disappeared.

"Can't we take him out of here? It's so dark, and the odor is terrible. He couldn't be any worse off lying on the ground."

Seth lifted Nelson without effort. He had wasted away until his body was only bones covered with a pasty skin. As Seth lowered him to the ground, Nelson's eyes opened.

"Dinah?" he whispered as he squinted at her.

"Yes, Dad. What happened to you? We looked and looked for you. Where have you been for these two years?"

"Has it been so long? Last I remember, I was sliding down a high bluff into a creek. When I awakened a few days ago, I thought I'd had a terrible nightmare."

He closed his eyes, and Seth said, "He's probably been out of his mind all this time."

"Do you think it's possible to take him to the hotel?"

"We'll have to try. The Indians can provide us with a carrier of some sort. The biggest problem is to find enough people who aren't superstitious about the *nahani* to carry him."

Without complaint Nelson endured the torture to his shriveled body as they carried him into Dawson. Seth helped Dinah bathe him and cut his tangled hair and whiskers. He pointed to another long scar on Nelson's forehead. "No doubt that's what caused his loss of memory. Poor man. Too bad we didn't find him before."

After they made him as comfortable as possible on the cot that Dixie had used, Dinah rushed to the hospital. She asked Sister Anne to check out Nelson's condition.

The nun brought some medication, but she couldn't diagnose Nelson's malady. "He's just wasted away. Probably he had pneumonia this past winter. I don't know what to do for him," she admitted.

They gave Nelson round-the-clock attention, and occasionally his mind cleared. Once he said, "Go back home, Dinah. I can't care for you now."

She told him that she loved Seth and wanted to stay with him, but she was never sure that Nelson understood her. He mumbled disconnected sentences, none that made any sense to either Seth or Dinah. He spoke Waldo's name often, and once he called out, "Waldo, I didn't think you'd do it."

Dinah had sent word to Waldo and Susie as soon as they brought her father to Dawson. Waldo had been Nelson's friend since his arrival in Oregon, and she knew Waldo would want to see him. Three days later, Susie came to the hotel.

"Where's Waldo?" Dinah demanded.

"He said he couldn't leave the mine just now. He'll be in next week, but I'm here to stay as long as you need me. A friend in need is a friend indeed. We've definitely decided to go back to Oregon to stay, but I'm not leaving when you're in trouble."

Susie's expert help did ease Dinah's duties, but in spite of their constant care, Nelson died. Dinah considered it a blessing that his death occurred in a clean room, rather than the terrible Indian dwelling, and she expressed her thanks to Jack for finding her father. She often thought of the debt she owed the Crows. What good friends they'd been. On the other hand, she was annoyed at Waldo, who didn't arrive in Dawson until after Nelson died.

They buried Nelson not far from where Dixie Belle was interred. Susie and Seth stood with Dinah during the brief ceremony. The mosquitoes swarmed from the swampy ground and buzzed around their heads, adding physical discomfort to Dinah's sorrowing spirit. In spite of her own grief, Dinah thought mostly of her grandparents and the letter she must write them.

In the days following his burial, she considered Nelson's request that she leave the North. Should she go to be with her grandparents to care for them in their old age? Their children were scattered throughout the States. But would she be willing to return to the calm life of the Pacific Northwest? Or was the lure of the Klondike too strong?

The yield from Dinah's mine had been so vast when the two men reached bedrock that if she invested her share of the gold wisely, she would have a good income for life. Seth and Vance, too, were accumulating fortunes. When the three of them discussed their options, they all agreed that they preferred to devote their future to the northland.

By midsummer, Dawson City was no longer a village. It had become a city containing two banks, two newspapers, five churches, telephones, electricity, running water, and steam heat. Although Seth and Dinah planned to send some of their gold with Susie and Waldo when they left the Yukon Territory, it was no longer necessary for miners to ship their own gold. The Canadian Bank of Commerce had brought in an assay plant, and they bought gold dust, making it more convenient to deposit their dust with a bank and let that institution have the worry of shipping it.

As summer progressed, Dawson looked more and more like an international city as people from all over the world converged on the area. The Mounted Police estimated Dawson's population at 18,000, with another 5,000 prospecting along the streams.

As they strolled the streets one August evening, Dinah said to Seth, "Isn't it a great experience to witness the growth of a city? When I think what these flats looked like when the Indians and I landed here only two years ago, I can't believe there's a city here now."

"I'm not sure it's changed for the better."

"You're nothing but a pessimist, Seth Morgan. Just look at all the amazing enterprises in Dawson now."

Not that she approved of many of the businesses, but Dinah did consider the growth of the city miraculous. False-fronted dance halls and gambling houses bore such names as the Pioneer, the Dominion, the Opera House, Monte Carlo, the Aurora, the Pavilion, the Mascot. Other buildings housed transport companies, outfitters, gold-dust buyers, dentists, lawyers, doctors, merchants, and dozens of mining exchanges.

Seth and Dinah stopped to watch a projectoscope flash pictures on a bedsheet screen, featuring American soldiers enroute to Manila and Gentleman Jim Corbett fighting to regain his heavyweight title.

Somewhere a portable organ wheezed out a tune, and Dinah recognized the words of a popular song, "I'm just a bird in a gilded cage."

On the sandbar along the Yukon, Wall Street and Broadway Avenue had been laid out. The variety of available goods amazed Dinah. Vendors hawked furs, the latest fashions from Paris, plug hats, shoes, jewelry, opera glasses, ice cream, dime novels, Bibles, and the works of Shakespeare. Men stood in line to have their fortunes told, their pictures taken, and their teeth filled with gold nuggets.

In spite of the vast influx of people, the town remained peaceful because the Mounted Police kept it that way. After Constantine left in June, Sam Steele had taken charge of Dawson. Bowing to the character of a frontier town, Steele didn't interfere with the saloons and gambling halls, and prostitution continued unchecked. But gun toting was forbidden, and cheating, disorderly conduct, and lurid behavior banned. The Mounties enforced the laws by handing down enormous fines and stiff penalties, the two main punishments being banishment from Dawson or hard labor on the government woodpile.

Sixty steamboats, eight tugboats, and twenty large barges operating in the area provided easy access to Dawson. Dinah often saw many people that she'd known in Portland.

"It is an amazing town," Seth admitted when they returned to the hotel, "but I'd grow weary of it if I had to live here."

"I like it. The most interesting people stay at the hotel, and they all have money to pay, unlike the ones I helped out last year."

Rising from her desk the next day to greet an elderly couple entering the hotel lobby, Dinah said, "May I help you?"

The brawny man with thick, crisp iron gray hair and glinting black eyes said, "Been digging up any more yards to find gold?"

Incredulously, Dinah said, "Uncle Matt?"

"Yes. Didn't know me, did you? And I hardly recognized you, sitting there like a lady. How you've changed!"

Dinah raced to throw her arms around Matt and his wife, Unity.

"What are you two doing up here?"

"Matt wanted to see what was going on. I had a hard time keeping him at home last summer, and nothing would do, but we had to come this year. We wanted to see Vance, too."

"He's busy digging gold. Come on back to my living room."

"Looks like you're doing all right, Dinah," Matt said.

Though he walked slowly, leaning on a cane, it was difficult to imagine that he was almost ninety years old.

"Yes, I am. Seth Morgan, whom you don't know, and Vance are working my claim as well as theirs, but I'm making a great deal of money in this hotel. I run a quiet place, and it's a favorite with the miners who dislike carousing. What do you think of our city?"

"From what I observed on our way from the wharf, it's worse than San Francisco in its heyday, and I didn't think anything could be worse than that."

"What's that big tent we saw on the other side of the river?" Unity asked.

"Oh, you mean our royal court! A couple of women— Mary Hitchcock and Edith Van Buren, seasoned world travelers—live there. This summer, rather than visit their favorite haunts in Europe or Asia, they're vacationing in Dawson City. It must have cost a small fortune to transport their cargo up the Yukon. They entertain the elite citizens of Dawson. As a hotel proprietor, I apparently don't fit in that class, for I haven't been invited, but I hear they serve delicacies like mock-turtle soup, asparagus salad with French dressing, ice cream, and French coffee."

"Wonder when we can visit the boy?" Matt asked.

"He isn't much of a boy now, Uncle, but I can take you to the mine today. When I first came here, we had to walk to the creeks, but there's a passable road now. I'll hire a carriage."

The sound of creaking windlasses carried to them on the wind as they approached Grand Forks at the junction of the Bonanza and the Eldorado. Twenty or more cabins, a few saloons, and two hotels marked the joining of the two golden rivers.

"This country has changed in two years," Dinah explained. "At first, timber covered these hills, undergrowth choked the valley floors, and the streams ran unfettered toward the Yukon. I'm glad I found gold, but I still hate to see the country denuded like this."

Vegetation had disappeared from the hills, now covered with newly washed gravel spewed from the miners' shafts. Cabins clustered over the benchlands surrounded by piles of rocks and clay. The streams, dammed and diverted into sluice boxes and tunnels, had become dumping grcunds for the miners' refuse.

Vance stuck his head out of the tunnel when their rig clattered into the mine site, and he shouted, "Gramps! Gran! Why didn't you let me know you were coming?"

He bounded to his grandparents and flung himself into Unity's arms, dirt and all. Pummeling his grandfather on the back, Vance said, "Am I glad to see you! Are you going to stay?"

"Not if I have anything to say about it," Unity laughingly answered. "I'm hoping this visit will cure Matt's yearnings to be young again."

While Vance took Matt on a tour of the diggings and to see Seth, Dinah invited Unity into the cabin. "I'll clean the place for them. It's never very tidy."

"Is this where you lived that first winter?"

"Yes, although it was existing rather than living." Dinah laughed at the remembrance. "I was so determined to prove that I could find gold that I shoveled gravel until I couldn't stand up, then I'd go to bed. Soon as I awakened, I'd start over again."

"It paid off, though," Unity reminded her.

"The gold itself soon lost its appeal for me. I only like gold for what I can do with it. I've been able to help many people this past winter, and if I hadn't had some finances, I couldn't have done it."

"Is Vance happy with this work?"

"Yes, but he does have a problem."

When Unity heard about Vance's love affair with Phoebe, she said, "Why do we always fall in love with the person who's the most difficult for us to have? When he knew that girl was in orders, why didn't he simply leave her alone?"

"Could you have let Uncle Matt go that easily?"

"No, I guess not. There was an instant spark between us

when we first met, and we've never changed. I suppose Vance is like us. Do you think there's any solution?"

"If the girl renounces her vows and marries Vance, he'll be happy, but I'm not sure that's best for Phoebe."

Matt and Unity stayed for a week, and before he left, Matt bought a quarter interest in a steamboat line with two vessels plying the Yukon between Whitehorse and Dawson. Vance and Seth came for dinner the last night before the Millers' departure.

Matt said to Vance, "I'm expecting you to keep an eye on my investment. I'm proud of how you're turning out. And you, too, Dinah. When you were children, I wouldn't have given a dime for either of you, but you've turned out pretty well."

"Do you consider this steamboat line a sound investment?" Seth asked. "Won't shipping between St. Michael and Dawson dominate the river traffic?"

"I doubt it. There's talk of a railroad being built from Skagway to Lake Bennett and eventually to Whitehorse. When the railroad is finished, that route will provide the quickest access to the Klondike."

"Will this go the way of other gold camps?" Unity asked. "Won't these people soon fade away, leaving Dawson a ghost town?"

Vance and Dinah stared at Unity, their mouths agape at the suggestion, but with the hint of a smile, Seth said, "It could happen, ma'am. For one thing, most of the men who came this summer realize that all the easy gold is gone. Many of them will leave before the freeze-up. When the easy money goes, so will the gamblers, the prostitutes, and the vendors. There's still a lot of gold in this country, but heavy equipment is needed to mine it."

"We've already had several outside companies wanting to buy our claims," Vance said.

"Do you intend to sell?"

"No, Gramps, Seth and I have decided to form a company ourselves. With our three claims and Waldo's, we think it will pay us to buy heavy equipment for deep-ground mining."

"But you surely don't think Dawson could become a ghost town?" Dinah said, her mind still on the amazing statement made earlier. "San Francisco didn't die."

"No, but many of the gold camps around Sacramento City are deserted now," Matt said. "If there's another big strike somewhere in this area, Dawson could be quickly evacuated."

"I don't believe it will die," Seth said, "because there's still gold to be mined, but the carnival atmosphere that we've had this summer won't last forever."

"I've been through all of this before, and I want to give the three of you some advice. In a gold strike, fortunes can be made and lost overnight—rich today and poor tomorrow. You've got a sure thing with what you have now. Don't gamble, don't overexpand, don't be greedy. Take what you have and be thankful for it. Put your priorities in order, and don't try to be Klondike kings, like those I've heard about since I've been here."

"I'm keeping that in mind, Matt," Seth said. "The saloons and the gambling halls are getting most of the gold. Men lose a fortune in one night at the faro table. Cheechakos and sourdoughs alike have taken to drinking."

"If Susie were here, she'd say, 'Easy come, easy go,' " Dinah said. "But you needn't worry about us, Uncle Matt. We have no yearning for any more gold strikes. Once is enough."

Dinah had been aware of the large Negro for several days. He appeared wherever she went, and one morning, when he loitered outside the hotel, she approached him.

"Is there something I can do for you? Are you looking for somebody?"

He removed his cap and flashed her a smile. "Yes, ma'am. I'm waiting for Seth Morgan to show up. Every place I've asked about him, they tell me to watch out at your place, that he comes here when he's in town."

"Are you Sam?"

"Yes 'um."

"He's been looking for you several months, so he'll be glad to know you're here. Where are you staying?"

"Got a tent down on the riverbank."

"I can direct you to the mine if you want to go, or I'll tell him you're here when he comes to town."

"I'll wait for him. I've had all the traveling I want, and I need to look around anyways."

Dinah had hoped that Sam wouldn't show up, but she supposed nothing could be settled between her and Seth until these two men found the killer they looked for. *And if they find him, what then? And who was the assassin? Hank Sterling? Joe Arthur?* Of all the thousands she'd met in the Klondike, Dinah couldn't think of any other possibilities.

Chapter Twelve

Fall and Winter 1898–99

W aldo and Susie arrived at the hotel a few days before their scheduled departure from the Klondike. Dinah arranged a farewell dinner for them, to which she invited Seth and Vance. Dinah had successfully stifled the anger she'd harbored against Waldo because he hadn't visited her father before his death. Waldo had been a good friend for years, and she determined not to allow that one unexplained incident to spoil their relationship.

The day of the dinner, Waldo and Susie disappeared for a few hours. Susie returned, laden with parcels, wearing a pink satin hat decorated with ostrich feathers. The huge hat appeared cumbersome, and it made Susie's squat, heavy figure seem shorter than usual.

" 'Fine feathers make fine birds,' " she quoted as Dinah stared at her in amazement. "Straight from Paris—or so I was told."

A smooth-shaven man entered the hotel lobby, and Dinah turned from her appraisal of Susie's finery. "May I help you, sir?"

The man flashed a large smile in her direction.

"Waldo!" she screamed. The heavy black beard had been shaved, leaving only a well-groomed mustache. Over his short haircut, he wore a black felt homburg. As Dinah had long suspected, Waldo looked at least ten years younger than Susie.

"Why, Waldo," she exclaimed, "you're a handsome man. Why have you kept your face covered all these years?"

"I thought gold miners were supposed to have whiskers," he joked. "Now that the Missus and I are headed Outside, I decided it was time to shave."

Waldo looked and acted like a man with a new lease on life, as if shedding the heavy whiskers had freed him from a mysterious past. Dinah followed them to their bedroom to see the new clothing.

"We've lived in rags for two years now, so we thought we might as well live it up. The folks in Oregon need to know we've struck it rich," Susie said.

"What are you going to do when you get home?"

"I don't intend to do anything except loll around in luxury."

"Yeah," Dinah jeered. "I don't believe that. You've worked too long to become lazy now."

With a mysterious look in his eyes, Waldo said, "My future is somewhat in doubt. I'm not making plans too far ahead."

Susie took Dinah's hand. "I wish you'd go with us, Dinah. I still feel responsible for you, although you've proved you can take care of yourself."

"I'll have Vance and Seth for company, so don't worry about me. Seth and I'll be married someday."

"Have you forgotten all your comments about proving your independence, not wanting a man to rule over you, and all that nonsense? Considering the nature of both you and Seth, I doubt you'll ever get along."

"We think we can. We've both accepted the other as we

are. And now that Seth has recommitted his life to God, I'm not worried about being his wife. Seth told me last week that he wanted our marriage to follow the biblical pattern outlined in the Book of Ephesians. I won't have any trouble submitting to a husband who loves me as Christ loved the church."

Most of the conversation during their evening meal concerned the mining that Seth and Vance would take over on Waldo's claim. After supper Vance disappeared quietly, and Dinah guessed he had a rendezvous with Phoebe.

Waldo said to Seth, "Let's take a walk around town. I doubt I'll ever be in Dawson again, and I want to have a last look at the city. Besides, the women probably want some time to themselves."

Seth and Waldo talked little as they ambled around the streets. They passed the new motion-picture theater and paused at a restaurant where a string orchestra played classical music. They pushed their way through crowds in front of saloons, dance halls, and gambling houses. They commented on the cheap, shabby buildings made elegant with carved cornices and pillars imitating foliage, shellwork, and scrolls. Emblazoned bay windows and wrought-iron balconies hinted of New Orleans.

In the saloons, bartenders, wearing starched shirts, aprons, and white waistcoats ornamented with diamond stickpins, served cocktails to their customers. At the gambling houses, faro, poker, dice games, and roulette wheels relieved miners of their fortunes.

Waldo turned down Paradise Alley, and Seth followed him, although he wasn't keen on being seen there, nor could he imagine why Waldo would want to remember the section of Dawson set aside for prostitutes. This street, directly behind a row of dance halls, housed a bevy of women living in a double line of identical frame shacks, each with a single window facing the narrow street. Although Waldo seemed to be looking for somebody, he was oblivious to the girls who stood invitingly in front of their shacks.

"When you come right down to it, Dawson's not a very pretty city, is it?" Seth said.

"No, and with all of this evil, it's bound to fail."

They walked for more than an hour, and since Seth couldn't see any point in prolonging good-byes, he started back toward the hotel.

"I haven't seen your black friend this evening. Maybe we should go down to his tent and check on him."

Nodding assent, Seth headed toward the Yukon. Sam sat beside a campfire, roasting a fish over glowing coals.

He flashed Seth a smile and then transferred his gaze to Waldo. The hand holding the fish stiffened, and Sam slowly lowered the fish into the fire, heedless when the meat began to sizzle. Sam stumbled to his feet and backed away, his eyes never leaving Waldo's face. He pointed a shaking hand at Waldo.

"It's him, Mister Seth," Sam whispered. "I ain't never forgot that face."

Amazed, Seth turned toward Waldo, surprised to find a slight smile on his features.

"I'm the man you've been looking for, Seth. I killed your daddy. I wasn't responsible for the death of Sam's father, but I did trigger the gun that ended Joseph Morgan's life. So your quest is over. I'm in your hands."

Seth had often wondered what he'd do if he came face-to-face with his father's killer, and now, trembling all over, he could only stare at Waldo. This man had been his friend for three years—a man with whom he'd shared a cabin, eaten at the same table, worked in his mine.

"But why reveal it now? If you hadn't shaved, you could have left the Klondike, and I'd never have known. Apparently you've been walking around all evening waiting for Sam to recognize you. Why not just tell me?"

Waldo shrugged his shoulders. "I suppose I was curious
to see if Sam would know me after eight years. And as to
why I didn't leave the Yukon without you knowing—I'm
tired of running away from what I did. I'd heard you were on
my trail. That's the reason I left Colorado and moved to
Oregon, and even though I'd changed my name and appearance, Oregon wasn't far enough away, either. I came to
Alaska, and you were here. I intended to go back to the
States immediately, but when you didn't suspect me, I
thought I was safe enough. I got rid of the items I'd taken
from your father. Then when you returned from Oregon and
said that Sam would be coming north, I knew I'd have to run
again."

Seth glared at Waldo, but he couldn't conjure up much
anger against the man.

"But it's also for your sake that I'm revealing myself to
you. I'm fond of you, Seth, and I don't want hatred and a
spirit of revenge to ruin your life."

Waldo sat on the log that Sam had vacated. "I came from
a religious family, and when I realized I'd killed your daddy,
who was a preacher, I decided I had to make restitution by
entering the ministry myself, but my spiritual efforts have
been a failure. God doesn't reward an unrepentant life. I
thought if I left the East, I wouldn't be confronted with my
deed any longer."

"But why did you kill him?"

"I served in the Confederate army, and like so many other
people in the South who couldn't accept defeat, I blamed the
freedmen for losing the war, and I hated anyone who helped
them. The Klan served as an outlet for my pent-up emotions,
and when I shot your daddy, it was in the heat of anger, as
if I were in battle again.

"Nelson didn't know anything about my past, but when
you told him about your father's death, he remembered that
I'd had a similar watch and gun."

"He didn't give one indication that he knew anything about that watch."

"Nelson was loyal to his friends, and he didn't want to betray me, but he threatened to tell you if I didn't confess. When he left to go prospecting, I followed him, and when we were quarreling, he fell off the cliff into the river."

Seth grabbed Waldo by the coat lapels and pulled him to his feet. "You mean you knew that and let Dinah wonder all those months about her father?"

"I thought he had drowned. I was distraught about it, for Nelson was my friend, but when I didn't speak up right at first, I decided it was too late. I've never had much courage, Seth."

Seth removed his hands and Waldo sank back to the log.

"I'm more inclined to forgive you for my father's death than for the worry you've caused Dinah."

"Nothing I knew would have relieved her worries. And I had Susie to think about."

"How much does she know?"

"Nothing!"

"It wasn't very admirable to marry a woman without telling her about your past."

Waldo smiled bleakly. "I've admitted that I'm a coward. Once you start on the road of deceit, Seth, it's easy to continue. Besides, I thought I'd buried my past." He stood again. "All right, you have me. What are you going to do with me? It's growing late."

Seth turned away from him and faced the swirling river. What could he do? He could fight with him, but it would be a one-sided fight, for he was younger and heavier than Waldo, and he had a feeling that Waldo wouldn't defend himself. He could shoot him, but if he did, would he be any better than Waldo? Besides, the Mounties would soon be on his trail, and he'd become a wanted man, running the way

Waldo had done for so many years. That would leave Dinah alone.

He could tell Susie about her husband's past, but she was happy with Waldo. Would he repay Susie's kindness to him by telling her she had married a murderer? He could have Waldo arrested and sent back to the States for trial, but a Klansman wouldn't be considered a criminal in South Carolina.

He had only one recourse, and that was to forgive Waldo and forget the injustice that had been done. The Bible said, "Vengeance is mine; I will repay, saith the Lord." Waldo would continue to suffer as he remorsefully contemplated the deaths of Joseph Morgan and Nelson Davis, and in his memories he would pay over and over for his crimes. Seth knew he'd been moving toward this decision for a long time, and that was the reason he could now renounce his vengeance.

Without going out of hearing, Seth wandered down the riverbank. Now that he'd learned the identity of his father's murderer, he found that his desire for revenge had lessened. Even so, Seth found it hard to throw off the burden he'd carried for so many years, and his feet dragged unwillingly as he returned to the campfire. The fish that Sam had intended for his supper had burned to a crisp, and the smoke from the campfire touched Seth's nostrils. Waldo stood quietly awaiting the verdict.

Seth's hand trembled as he extended it to this friend, who was also his enemy. "I forgive you, Waldo, and I pray that God will forgive you, too."

Their hands clasped, and tears came to Waldo's eyes. "I don't intend to tell Dinah that I may have caused her father's death. You can do as you like, but please wait until I leave. Nelson Davis was the best friend I ever had, and I'll never forgive myself."

"I won't tell her."

"And, Seth, let me advise you to make your own peace with God. From my experience, I know that the way of the transgressor is hard. You've forgiven me; now let God forgive you for your waywardness."

Seth nodded, his heart too full for speech. He watched Waldo walk hurriedly toward town, no longer going with the slouch he'd affected for years. He walked like a free man.

Sam moved to Seth's side. "You done right, Mister Seth. Killing him wouldn't solve nothing."

"I realize that now, but at least I know who killed Dad. I thank you for helping me, and I'll make it worth your while. What will you do now?"

"Head south. I ain't hankerin' to stay in this Klondike during the winter."

"Don't go on the boat with Waldo, but before you leave, I'll give you enough gold to take you where you want to go. I'll arrange with my bank here to give you a bill of credit at some bank in the States. I believe in standing by my friends, and you've been a friend, Sam."

"If I see your mama, what you want me to tell her?"

"Tell her I'm coming to see her, Sam. I'm coming home."

Dinah's last link with childhood severed when she gave Susie a final hug and watched her board the steamboat that would take the Knights to the States. Soon a new life would begin for Dinah, because she'd committed her future to Seth, who this morning had asked her to marry him. It seemed as she waved to Susie that this day marked the final break with Nelson Davis and her childhood.

They watched until the steamboat faded from view, and when they turned toward the town, a cold blast of air caused Dinah to shiver.

"We're facing another Klondike winter," she said. "I wonder how terrible this one will be?"

Seth didn't answer, and she sensed his preoccupation.

He'd told her that he no longer sought his father's assassin and that he had trusted his future to God. To Dinah, it was obvious that Seth had withheld information from her concerning his change of heart, but she wouldn't pester him about it. Someday he would tell her. For now, she contented herself with the security of his love.

Though Dinah thought she was done with good-byes, a few weeks later Timothy came to the hotel. She hadn't seen Timothy often since she'd told him that she intended to marry Seth, and she greeted him warmly.

"I've come to say good-bye. I'm being transferred to main headquarters at Ottawa."

"At least you will miss another winter here, but I regret having you leave, Timothy. You've been a true friend, and I appreciate all you've done for me."

She extended her hand, and Timothy held it tightly and lowered his lips to her palm. "I asked for the transfer, Dinah. I don't want to appear a poor loser, but I'd rather not live here and see you married to another man."

"I understand, Timothy. I pray you'll have a happy future. You deserve it."

To stifle her sorrow over Susie's departure and the loss of Timothy's friendship, Dinah spent more time helping Father Judge at the hospital. With typhoid, pneumonia, and dysentery debilitating the townspeople, the little hospital was full, and the priest housed patients on the roofless second floor of the hospital, but the rain held until the roof was completed.

When Seth came for a visit, Dinah shared her concern for the priest. "He will not take care of himself," she said. "We try to get him to rest, but he's constantly on the go. I wonder if he ever sleeps, for Phoebe says they have orders to call him at any hour if someone asks to see him."

"I met him on the street as I entered town, and he seemed so frail that a good puff of wind could blow him over."

"Have you heard that the people of Dawson are planning a benefit show on Christmas to pay off the debt on his hospital? It's a minstrel show and will be held at the Tivoli Theater."

"The priest won't like it."

"I know, but he'll be glad to have his hospital debt free. They're also taking up donations to buy a new set of clothing for him."

"I'll come in for the show, if you want to go."

"Yes, please do, and tell Vance to come for Christmas Day if both of you can get away."

"Most of the cheechakos have left the country now, so our claims will be safe enough. We'll be here on the twenty-fourth."

"They're expecting a full house at the minstrel show," Dinah told Seth and Vance when they gathered around the table in her private dining room on Christmas afternoon. She had earlier fed more than one hundred miners, free of charge, in the main dining room.

"We brought our town clothes with us," Vance said. "We guessed this would be a dress affair since Dawson is becoming sophisticated."

"Phoebe whispered to me yesterday that a few of the nuns are coming to the show, since it's in Father Judge's honor. So you will want to look your best."

Dinah smiled at the light that leaped into Vance's eyes.

"What did Judge think of his new clothing?" Seth asked.

"He refused them politely, telling the donors that as a Jesuit priest he wasn't allowed to accept gifts. They'd bought a sealskin coat, cap and gloves, besides a new robe. He finally took them, and I think he agreed to wear them tonight, but I doubt that he'll have them on tomorrow."

Vance disappeared when they reached the theater, and Dinah figured he'd gone to find Phoebe. Dinah and Seth sat hand in hand to watch the show. A dozen participants gathered in a semicircle on the stage. The master of ceremonies exchanged jokes with several of the main characters. The presentation contained a few comedy routine dances and some sentimental songs. The last part of the show was a one-act skit portraying the antics of a cheechako's first days in gold country.

When the emcee called Father Judge the grand old man of Dawson, the miners applauded wildly, and Father Judge was finally forced to the platform. The audience cheered during a standing ovation of more than five minutes. Through her tears, Dinah smiled at the priest, who endured with dignity what must have been an embarrassing moment for him.

After Christmas the temperature plummeted to fifty below zero, and the health of the priest also took a nosedive. He contracted pneumonia, and the sisters held little hope for his recovery. Seth went to visit him with the intent of encouraging the priest to better health.

He received Seth with a smile, and his face beamed with a radiant light. "I am dying, my friend."

When Seth tried to jolly him out of this attitude, the priest continued. "I am dying, and I don't know that I have any reason to live except that there's no one else to carry on my work. The nuns will take care of the hospital, but who will go into the hinterland to minister to the lonely, the sick, and the dying?"

"God will provide a replacement if you die."

"Perhaps you?"

"I don't know. Perhaps."

"I pray that it will be so. We've been friends since you came to this country, Seth, and I have agonized over your lack of faith."

"But God has restored my faith. I've watched you and have been inspired. I've observed Dinah, who may be worth a quarter of a million dollars, come here and work in these wards day after day, simply for the joy of helping those in need. I want the same peace and serenity in my life that the two of you have. It will be worth my fortune to have it."

"You can have it, my friend." Opening the Bible lying at his side, Judge read in his weak voice, " 'But rather seek ye the kingdom of God; and all these things shall be added to you. . . . Sell that ye have, and give alms; provide yourselves bags which wax not old, a treasure in the heavens that faileth not, where no thief approacheth, neither moth corrupteth. For where your treasure is, there will your heart be also.' " Gasping for breath, he handed the Bible to Seth. "Read Matthew thirteen, verses forty-five and forty-six."

With difficulty, Seth read, " 'Again, the kingdom of heaven is like unto a merchant man, seeking goodly pearls: Who, when he had found one pearl of great price, went and sold all that he had, and bought it.' "

"My friend, if you've truly found the pearl of great price, you'll sacrifice everything else to keep it. To accept God's will for your life is the pearl you should seek."

Father Judge died two days later, and Seth and Dinah stood with hundreds of other Dawson residents at his gravesite. The priest would have been horrified to know that his remains rested in a casket that cost over a thousand dollars. During the three days it took to dig his grave in the frozen soil, Dawson residents mourned the man who had given his life for them.

The day after his funeral, Phoebe appeared at Dinah's hotel, carrying her few possessions in a pillowcase.

"I've left for good. I couldn't desert Father Judge, but now that he's gone, I have decided on the break. I talked to Sister Anne, who is sympathetic to my situation and encouraged me to leave. I couldn't help wonder if in her youth she hadn't been in love, too."

"Quite possibly. What do you want me to do now?"

"Send word to Vance. We'll be married right away. He's been waiting for me."

"Are you willing to live in a log cabin at the mine?"

With a smile, Phoebe said, "You've seen my quarters at the hospital. His cabin couldn't be worse than what I've lived in for months. But he's promised that we'll add another room to the cabin." Dinah was pleased to realize that Vance had been so far-reaching in his plans. She still thought of him as a boy, but in the Klondike people matured rapidly.

Vance and Phoebe married a week later, and after they left for the cabin, Seth stayed behind to talk to Dinah.

"Dinah, I want us to be married as soon as possible, but I think I should be frank with you about my plans for the future."

"Whatever they are, I want to share them."

"The death of Father Judge made quite an impact on me. Although I'm not of his faith, I had a great respect for him and what he was doing. Then I've thought of your father and Waldo, men with a vision of spreading the gospel in this area."

"Now that they're gone, no one seems available to take their place."

"That's the way I feel. Although several churches have sprung up in Dawson, no one displays any missionary zeal, the kind that's needed to go into the highways and hedges to alert the natives and miners of their need to serve God. I've read Isaiah's vision over and over, recalling God's words, 'Whom shall I send, and who will go for us?' If I answer that call, 'Here am I, send me,' will you go with me?"

"I'm willing. How do you propose to do it?"

"I've made a fortune in the North. I'd like to spend it to build a school for the natives, or by having a preaching mission in the back country."

"This hotel would make a good boarding school for native

youth, and I'd be willing to use it for that. Jack and Nannie will help us, I'm sure."

"I don't know what way the Lord will lead us, but whichever way it is, we'll be together."

"Let's go to Oregon for our wedding, so my grandparents can be there. Vance and Phoebe can look after our property."

"I agree, and although it will take a long time, I want to return to South Carolina for a visit. My mother must be told about Janice Sue's death, and I've not been able to put it in a letter. Let's visit our families and then come back here, either to Alaska or the Yukon Territory."

"We'll go as soon as the spring thaw. I've loved you for three years, Seth, but I didn't suppose you'd ever love me in return. You always treated me as if I were a child."

"How else could I treat you when you acted childish?"

Dinah pulled away from his arms, and her blue eyes sparkled angrily. "Seth Morgan," she started, but Seth laughed and stopped her fiery retort with his lips. She forgot her anger in the passion of his long kiss.

Lifting his head, Seth caressed the blond hair tumbling around her face, and his eyes left no doubt of his love for her.

"I suppose I must stop treating you as a child. There's no doubt you're a woman now."

Epilogue

*D*awson was the scene of several disastrous fires, the worst of them occurring on the night of April 26, 1899. Over one hundred buildings were destroyed, with a loss totaling more than a million dollars. The town began to rebuild at once, and although that summer saw a great influx of people, Dawson never again attained the glamour of the fabulous year of 1898.

Early in 1899, vague rumors filtered through the northland of a new gold strike on Norton Sound near the mouth of the Yukon River. Although hearers scoffed at this news, miners drifted away from the Klondike. At first only a few left, but as the reports became more positive, Dawson emptied, just as Fortymile and Circle City had done when news of the Bonanza strike circulated.

When it was confirmed that the sands of Nome, Alaska, were producing fortunes, gold mania caught on, and Dawson was on its way downhill. More than 8,000 left Dawson in a single week. Ironically, almost three years from the day George Carmack staked his claim on the Bonanza, the Klondike stampede came to an end.

But the Klondike gold rush stands out as one of the most unusual of the world's stampedes. At least 100,000 started out for the Klondike, and 40,000 of those reached Dawson, However, less than half of that number prospected, and only about 4,000 found gold. Though a few hundred accumulated large fortunes, only a small percentage of them kept their wealth. Historians consider the stampede as one of the most futile mass movements in the history of mankind, for the gold fields of the Yukon Territory never produced as much money as the total amount expended by the cheechakos of 1897–1898.

Although the major characters in this book are fictitious, the following people played important roles in the Klondike gold rush: Charles Constantine, Bill Ogilvie, William McPhee, George Carmack, Skookum Jim, Tagish Charley, Joseph Ladue, Father William Judge, Henry Ash, Arthur Walden, Alex McDonald, and Sam Steele.

Suggested Reading

*F*or further reading on this fabulous era in American history, see:

Berton, Pierre. *The Klondike Fever.* New York: Alfred Knopf, 1958.

Martinsen, Ella Lung. *Black Sand and Gold.* Portland, Oregon: Binford and Mort Publishing, 1956.

Martinsen, Ella Lung. *Trail to North Star Gold.* Portland, Oregon: Binford and Mort Publishing, 1969.

May, Robin. *The Gold Rushes.* London: William Luscombe Publisher, Ltd., 1977.

Place, Marian T. *The Yukon.* New York: Ives Washburn, Inc., 1967.